Of Minds and Hearts

Of Minds and Hearts

C. Dean A. Papas

Imprint Books

Copyright © 2003 C. Dean A. Papas
All rights reserved.

ISBN 1-59109-609-X

Of Minds and Hearts

PROLOGUE

What is the compelling force that drives someone later in life to write a novel? I don't really know. Maybe in the course of living forgotten experiences and observations became stored images; when reentered into consciousness were found to be interesting, intriguing, and inspiring.

Novels and fiction are not completely devoid of reality. The events never really happened, but as the characters develop, think, feel, act, and react with each other, exhibit human strengths and weaknesses that we see in ourselves and those surrounding us every single day.

The core of the story has been in and out of my mind for many years. It comes back periodically and additions and deletions were made, but no notes were kept. With plenty of time on my hands at this period of my life, I made the decision to write this novel.

From early on, as we grow up, we are conditioned to relate all thoughts, intellectual, and cognitive functions to our minds, and all sentiments and feelings to our hearts, good or bad.

"This man or woman is really smart. What a quick mind." Or, "what a sick mind to even think of something so dirty."

"This man or woman was heartbroken after his wife or her husband died. They were so much in love." Or, "there is nobody I know of with so much hatred in his or her heart."

Minds and hearts can independently chart their own courses and if they do cross paths could be by chance and not by intent or design.

The depth, maturity, and character of an individual depends on if, how, and when the mind and the heart communicate. If minds and hearts don't work in tandem and compliment each other, happiness would be elusive, with possible disaster in the making.

Mothers have killed their children-Medea. Children have killed their mothers-Electra. Husbands, still in love, have killed their wives-Othello. Drama, as an art form, simply imitates life.

The story is fiction, but the minds and the hearts are real, and so could be the protagonists in anyone's life play.

C. Dean A. Papas

To
The Minds and the Hearts, past, present, and future, known and unknown, who by working in harmony have enriched humanity with Knowledge, Wisdom, Innovation, Ethics, Science, Art, Love, Charity, Respect, Compassion, Sacrifice, Freedom, Family, Civility, Justice, Goodness, Value, and Virtue.

CHAPTER ONE

HAPPINESS TO TRAGEDY

If you saw Jim Woodman in an elevator, supermarket, or department store, you would take a second look at him instinctively, especially if you were a woman. Jim's thick but symmetrical eyebrows, prominent high cheekbones, square jaw and a well-matched straight bridge nose definitely depicted a masculine face. His medium length black hair parted in the middle, covered the very top of his ears. His unusual lighter color skin, even for a white man, softened his features and made his facial expressions more aristocratic and gentle.

Jim, in the eyes of a professional photographer, wouldn't be perceived as model 'handsome' or 'sexy,' but definitely photogenic. He was lean, six feet tall, his body language was restrained but deliberate, and his demeanor emanated self-confidence, strong will, intelligence; a person of character and values.

Jim, an investment consultant, worked for the banking industry following his graduation from college, while he got his MBA in international finance. His interest was in investments in emerging industries within the European Union market that were attractive to institutional investors in U.S.

The company Jim worked for the past five years had its headquarters in the U.S. and operated two large overseas offices; one in London and the other in Brussels. Jim visited the overseas operations several times for combined corporate meetings and strategic planning, but never stayed long enough for any sightseeing. Jennifer, Jim's wife, joined him once, but the pace was very hectic that left very little time for them to have any fun.

Jennifer, five feet two inches tall, was a petite woman but carried her small, well-proportioned body with grace and elegance. Her refined and delicate facial features, shining, free-flowing shoulder length brown hair, beautiful deep blue eyes and arresting smile transcended an ethereal quality. Jennifer was reassuring, supportive, compassionate, and loving to all. A smile, handshake, or hug from Jennifer could change your gloomy day to sunshine. She was articulate, spoke softly with conviction and wisdom, and never overbearing. When you looked at her you wouldn't think of her physical beauty at all. Jennifer epitomized the beauty from within. If angels were living on earth among us mortals, Jennifer would be one of them.

Jim and Jennifer met in college, when he was in the first year of his MBA program and she was a junior. They got married after graduation. Their union, everybody thought, was made in heaven, and the romance seemed to last forever.

Jim came from a stable middle class family, but regretted the fact that he was an only child. Jennifer's background was similar to Jim's with the exception that her growing up years were enriched with a brother and a sister. Jim was accepted by Jennifer's family as another son and brother and was elated, making up for lost time doing silly things brothers and sister do during their adolescent years.

Jim and Jennifer felt very secure about their marriage, both emotionally and financially, and wanted to start a family.

Jim had been promoted twice, each time with a substantial raise, and Jennifer was ready to quit her CPA job as soon as she got pregnant. Her accounting firm was aware of her intentions, and very supportive. Jennifer's performance with the firm was outstanding. Her clear and inventive mind combined with a loving heart made her a natural leader. For the past two years she was the director of one of the divisions, supervising twelve accountants, with all the attached ancillary personnel. Everybody, in Jennifer's office, knew that she had been trying to get pregnant for the last three years. She and Jim had recently undergone extensive work-up to rule out any causes of sterility. If Jennifer had to undergo any type of treatment she was ready to quit working.

When Jennifer returned from lunch, she was surprised to find on her desk a dozen yellow roses in a crystal vase and a large red envelope. She opened the envelope and pulled out a red card. In gold calligraphy the message said, 'We love you and value you.' She opened the card and the inside was blank except for a hand written message that said, 'Jennifer, please come to my office as soon as you are back. Jeff.'

Jennifer opened her mouth wide, took a deep breath, and sat down. The card was made to order, and the yellow roses looked beautiful in the Baccarat vase. Jeff Goldstone was the managing partner of the accounting firm. He had held the position for the last six years. During his tenure the firm had doubled in size and contracted with several big and important corporate clients. Jeff was in his early sixties, slightly stocky, with short white hair. He was formal, demanding but fair, honest and open, with very little tolerance for excuses. He accepted mistakes only once, provided they became learning tools.

Jennifer opened her purse, touched up her make up, and felt composed enough to walk to Jeff's office, located at the end of a long hallway. When Jennifer walked to his secretary's desk, she was greeted with,

"Good afternoon Mrs. Woodman, Mr. Goldstone is expecting you."

"Good afternoon to you, too, Irene. And next time, please call me by my first name."

Irene knocked at Jeff's door.

"Mr. Goldstone, Mrs. Woodman is here."

"Come right in," he replied. Irene opened the door and Jennifer walked in. Jeff got up, took Jennifer's right hand and held it with both of his.

"Nice to see you Jennifer, please sit down." Then he said to Irene,

"Please hold all my calls. Tell them I am tied up in a meeting with one of the directors."

Irene walked out of Jeff's office and closed the door behind her. Jeff pulled up a chair and sat across from Jennifer.

"Jennifer, I have the greatest admiration for you. I know, emotionally this is a very difficult time in your life, and how important is for you and Jim to have a baby. I have been in this business long enough and I have seen first hand how one's emotions and family situations can compromise performance and productivity.

You have been like a rock in this firm, and a stabilizing force. You move through pettiness and employees complaints with finesse, understanding, and fairness. You are a delicate and a beautiful woman; you can make sound decisions with credibility, that men four times your size won't."

Jennifer felt uncomfortable and embarrassed.

"Mr. Goldstone, I am flattered, but I think you exaggerate quite a bit. There are many employees that deserve credit for my success."

"Of course, that's what a fair leader would say," he remarked.

"Jennifer, I am a selfish man. Employees with your character, expertise, and most of all trust come once in a lifetime. I hate to lose you. I hope you have a baby soon, but a professional of your caliber will need some stimulation. Maybe sometime in the future, even with a small child staying at home, you could give us a few hours a week. I will personally choose the work, and no deadlines. The office courier will deliver and pick up the files when ready. Bill the firm on an hourly basis for your work, and baby-sitting expenses, if you need somebody to watch the baby, while you are working."

Jennifer smiled.

"Mr. Goldstone, you are talking about a baby, and I am not even pregnant yet."

"Don't worry. Medicine is so advanced nowadays. It took

one of my nieces eight years, and now she has two kids. By the way, the firm will keep all your benefits active, including your life insurance and 401(k)."

"Mr. Goldstone, you are so generous, and I am very thankful to the firm, and especially to you. I know somewhere down the line I would go back to work. I would like to reassure you that my loyalty belongs to this firm and nowhere else."

"That's what I like to hear."

Both got up; Jennifer walked to the door, and Jeff opened and held the door for her.

"Mr. Goldstone the roses are beautiful, and what a vase. You have an impeccable taste."

"A lady like you deserves the best. Say hello to Jim from me. Goodbye Jennifer."

"Goodbye Mr. Goldstone, have a nice afternoon, and thanks for everything."

Jennifer was literally flying going back to her office. It was nice to be appreciated and complemented by a man of Jeff's stature. His idea to do some work from the house wasn't a bad one. But right now her whole energy was geared to having a baby, not only for herself, but for Jim as well. He was so ready to become a father as much as she was ready to become a mother. Jim was more verbal than she. He, having been an only child, subconsciously when a baby came might go back in time and play with a little brother or sister he never had. The innocence and playfulness of a child could transpose an adult into a childlike state, reminiscing of past carefree times, and the abandon of childhood.

Tomorrow was a big day for the Woodmans. They had a 4 o'clock appointment with Dr. Cook, Jennifer's gynecologist, to discuss the results of the tests.

It was 6 o'clock in the morning; the alarm went off in the Woodmans' bedroom.

Jim got up very quietly, turned the alarm off, walked to the bathroom, brushed his teeth, and started shaving. Shortly,

Jennifer woke up, stretching and yawning, looked at the clock and yelled,

"Jim, it's 6 o'clock. Why are you up so early?"

Jim came out of the bathroom, with his face full of soap holding his razor. "Jennifer, I have to leave the office at 3 o'clock. We have an appointment with Dr. Cook at 4 o'clock. I have a very busy day, and I would like to start early."

"Oh my goodness. How in the world could I have forgotten?"

"Go back to sleep. I will come back to kiss you goodbye before I leave."

Jim went back to the bathroom, finished shaving and washing up, returned to the bedroom, and started getting dressed. Jim, every night before going to bed, laid out the suit, shirt, tie, socks, and shoes he was to wear next day.

Looking dapper, and with his usual expression of confidence, Jim went to Jennifer to kiss her goodbye in his usual routine. First on the eyes saying, "your deep blue eyes give me hope," then on the lips, "your smile promises me happiness," and last on the left chest, "your heart fills mine with love."

"I have a good feeling love, everything is going to be all right. I will see you this afternoon. Bye, I love you."

It was 3:50 in the afternoon.

Jim was sitting in the main lobby, where Dr. Cook's office was located, waiting for Jennifer. Shortly, the door connecting the garage to the lobby opened and Jennifer walked in. Jim took Jennifer by the left hand and asked her,

"Did you have hard time finding parking? This place is so busy with so many physicians in the building."

"Not at all. As a matter of fact, I parked four spaces down from where you parked. I saw your car."

Jim and Jennifer took the elevator to the fifth floor. Still holding hands entered Dr. Cook's waiting room and walked to Veronica's desk, Dr. Cook's secretary. "Good afternoon Mr. and

Mrs. Woodman. Dr. Cook is expecting you. Please follow me, I will take you to his office."

Jim and Jennifer followed Veronica and as soon as she opened the door, Dr. Cook, in his mid fifties, bald, a little rotund and a happy-go-lucky character, greeted them in his usual jolly and exuberant manner.

"Hi kids? How are you doing? Isn't it fun trying to have a baby? Please sit down."

The seriousness and preoccupation on on Jim and Jennifer's faces melted down miraculously and both cracked up.

Dr. Cook sat on his desk chair, across from Jim and Jennifer.

"It's nice to see you guys laughing. You don't want to have a baby with a gloomy, stony, and sad face. Do you? Of course, not. Jim, let's start with you. Your sperm count and motility are normal, and you will have no problem fathering a child.

Jennifer, all your tests were with normal range except for one."

Jennifer became teary, took a hanky out of her purse and wiped her eyes. Jim put his arm around her, and whispered in her ear,

"Please, don't make sad my deep blue beautiful eyes of hope."

Dr. Cook looked Jennifer directly in the eyes and continued,

"Jennifer, please don't cry, and hear me out. Two weeks ago, you had a test done at the x-ray department of the hospital. The name of the test is hystero-salpingogram. The radiologist placed a small catheter in the opening of the cervix that is part of the uterus, and injected dye to examine the cavity of the uterus, and the tubes that connect to your ovaries to your uterus.

Let me explain to you now, what a woman's body needs to conceive besides her husband's sperm. a) Normal ovaries. Your menstrual cycle is regular, and your ovaries function normally. b) Normal uterus. Your uterus is normal, and full pregnancy can be carried out without any problem. c) Open fallopian tubes.

The tubes that connect the ovaries to the uterus, and allow the egg to travel to the uterus to meet the sperm for conception.

If you recall, when you were eleven years old, your appendix burst, and you developed severe peritonitis of the abdomen and pelvis, that scarred and blocked your tubes. The test showed your fallopian tubes are closed. Despite this problem you can become pregnant and have a baby."

Jim and Jennifer appeared relaxed for the first time and looked at each other smiling.

"Jennifer, your problem can be overcome with 'in vitro fertilization' known as a test tube baby. Under anesthesia an instrument called laparoscope will be inserted into your abdominal cavity and eggs will be retrieved from your ovaries. Your eggs will be fertilized with Jim's sperm, kept frozen, and after preparation, will be implanted in your uterus. The rate of success with each implantation is about thirty percent, and this is the reason several eggs are fertilized. I have already made all the arrangements with the University Fertility Center. Veronica will hand you all the information. Once your pregnancy has been confirmed, the Center will refer you back to me for prenatal care and delivery. Do you have any questions?"

"Dr. Cook, you are so thorough that everything is clear in my mind."

"I like your sense of humor, too," Jim said.

"You made us relax. No wonder your patients love you."

"Oh my goodness, Jennifer, I forgot something very important to tell you. Please forgive me, I am so sorry."

"And what is that Dr. Cook," Jennifer asked with some concern.

"This is a must. If you have a boy, you name him after me, John and if you have a girl, you name her after me, Joanna," Dr. Cook said laughing.

Jennifer, her eyes sparkling with joy, hugged and kissed Dr. Cook on both cheeks. She and Jim said goodbye to Dr. Cook and Veronica gave Jennifer a large brown envelope with all information and instructions concerning her appointment with the University Fertility Center.

"Mrs. Woodman, stop worrying. Dr. Cook referred two patients last year and both became pregnant. One is due in three months."

"Thanks for everything Veronica, and I hope to see you soon."

Jim opened the door, let Jennifer out, then he followed her and closed the door behind him. Once outside the office, Jim lifted Jennifer by the waist, and with her face touching his said,

"Love, thanks God, we are going to have a baby. Our love and lives are going to be complete. I love you so much, Jennifer."

"I love you, too. I can sense your yearning to become a father. I have the same feeling. We are so blessed. Please let me down, you will hurt your back."

"You give me so much joy baby. Don't you know angels can fly? When I hold you, you take all the weight away from me."

Jim and Jennifer kissed several times, then Jim with care and affection, let Jennifer body slowly slide over his to the floor, as if she were the most precious being in the whole Universe.

Jim walked Jennifer to her car, waited and waved at her until she was gone, then he went to his car and drove away.

Almost ten months went by since Jennifer was referred to the University Fertility Center.

Veronica, Dr. Cook's secretary, opened today's mail and sorted his professional correspondence. One of the letters was from the Fertility Center provided an updated progress note to Dr. Cook concerning Jennifer's treatment. It stated that two fertilized eggs had been implanted and failed. A third attempt was made two months ago.

Poor Mrs. Woodman, Veronica thought, *She wants a baby so bad. I hope she is not disappointed and remains optimistic.*

A few minutes later the phone rang, and she answered.

"This is Dr. Cook's office, Veronica speaking, may I help you?"

"Hi Veronica, this is Dr. Herman. Is Dr. Cook in the office?"

"Yes sir, he is. Please wait, I will get him."

Veronica got up in hurry and went to Dr. Cook's office.

"Dr. Cook, Dr. Herman from the Fertility Center is on line 2. Would you please pick up the call?"

"Thanks Veronica."

Dr. Cook pushed the flashing lighted button on line 2, and picked up the hand set.

"Hi Bob, this is John. How are you? Two weeks ago I came to the Center for Grand Rounds, but I didn't see you, you were out of town for a conference. What is new?"

"Well, John, I have great news for you. We finally made it. Your patient Jennifer Woodman is pregnant. She was in my office early this morning, and got the great news. She was elated, crying and laughing at the same time. She is about eight weeks and the first sonogram, which was done today, looks great. I don't have to see her any more. I advised her to see you in about two weeks to start her prenatal care."

"That's great news for the Woodmans. They are such a nice couple, loving, and devoted to each other. You did a great job as usual, you are one of the best."

"John wasn't as easy. The first and second implant failed; fortunately the third and the last fertilized egg available at this time progressed into a successful gestation."

"Bob, thanks again. Let's get together for lunch sometime soon. It's on me. Let me know when you are free. Goodbye for now."

Dr. Cook hung up smiling, then became pensive and started thinking. *Intervening with nature has been always controversial, and a point of debate among ethicists, religious leaders, sociologists, economists and even politicians. Did we play God or fool Mother Nature in Jennifer's case? Did the All Mighty gave us the wisdom to be His facilitators in creating life? Are we co-creators or co-gods? Have we appointed ourselves 'Defacto Trustees' of Mother Nature? These questions would be with us in perpetuity beyond the boundaries of intellectual curiosity, personal philosophies, religious convictions, and scientific achievements. What was accomplished in Jennifer's case took years of research and unprecedented investment in both human and financial resources.*

Most, if not all, Health Insurance companies, due to the tremendous costs involved, wouldn't cover or pay for Jennifer's procedure. The argument is, failure to conceive is not an illness, or something that puts your health at risk. The in vitro fertilization procedure is listed under 'Exclusions.'

If the Woodmans couldn't pay themselves, their dream and desire to have a child would have never been possible. Now the question for ethicists, religious leaders, sociologists, economists, and politicians is, if God or human intelligence gave us the wisdom and privilege to fool Mother Nature and facilitate the creation of life, were any financial stipulations built in? Capable, moral, productive, of no-means couples yearning for a child are to be denied the joy of parenthood because they cannot pay? On the other hand, is society (insurance) responsible for paying for couples who can't have children? If society does not pay, is it ethical to follow the free market distribution law of 'economic rationing,' where goods and services are available only to those who can afford them? Is a child a commodity or a being created in the image of God, with a mind and a heart like ours?

Dr. Cook got up, stretched, took a few steps, then sat down again.

Life can be so complex many a time, he thought, *but at least thinking about its complexities changes our level of awareness.*

Jennifer left the Fertility Center in a state of incalculable level of elation. She drove home very carefully, with both hands on the wheel.

Her unattended tears of happiness flowing out of her deep blue eyes and running over her naturally rosy cheeks, made her entire face glow, as the early autumn sun caressed her moist skin. When the tears reached and wetted her lips, the salty taste felt by her tongue was like honey. Tears of happiness are the sweetest of all. Jennifer was so blessed. She was in love with the most beautiful man in all dimensions - Physical, intellectual, spiritual. She was in love with man with a great mind and a golden heart. Today she was blessed again. Her dream to have a baby came true. Jennifer thought, *Why do I have everything and others have very little or nothing at all? Am I better than others? Absolutely, not. Do I deserve it all? I don't know. That's the mystery of life, I guess. I am thankful to God for everything, and especially for my baby.*

She drove directly home from the Fertility Center and arrived about 11 o'clock. She parked the car and came inside the house for the first time knowing she was pregnant.

Jennifer was overwhelmed. She went to the living room, sat on the sofa, put her purse on the coffee table, took her shoes and her jacket off, got up and started dancing, twirling, jumping, and singing;

"I am going to have a baby, I am going to have a baby, oh no, we are going to have a baby. I better call Jim right now to give him the good news."

Jennifer went to the kitchen, picked up the phone and called Jim.

"Jim...Jim," Jennifer sat down and started crying.

"What is wrong Angel?" Jim asked in a soothing, affectionate, and concerned voice.

"Jim, nothing is wrong. As matter of fact, never has anything been so right. I saw Dr. Herman at the Fertility Center at 8:30 this morning for a follow up visit after the third implant. I am sorry I didn't tell you, I didn't want you to be disappointed again."

"Jim...Jim," Jennifer started sobbing;

"We made it...we made it...we are going to have a baby. I am eight weeks pregnant. I had my first sonogram and everything looks great, Dr. Herman said."

"Oh my God, thanks. What a monumental and victorious day in our lives," Jim said, as tears filled his eyes.

"I love you so much, Jennifer, but now I love you double, since you carry the other love of our lives. Our happiness and love will be forever and with no limits. You are the most beautiful mother to be in the entire world. The sparkle and the glow in your eyes and the smile in your face will outshine even the brightest stars of all constellations."

Jennifer, drying her eyes with Kleenex tissue, tried to regain her composure.

"Jim you know how much I love you. Our lives are so unique. We are not only married and lovers, but also each other's best friend. I never imagined that our journey in this world would be so perfect. Our personal shortcomings and imperfections vanished to oblivion, once we were united to a perfect fit. Each of us carried half the pieces of a puzzle that we couldn't finish alone, ever. Together we made it."

"Your metaphor is so well taken and suited for us," Jim remarked.

"It shows the depth of your understated wisdom."

"Jim, I like to do something special today to celebrate the new beginning. And what could be more appropriate than to start building the nest for our baby, starting the nursery. I am going to Park Plaza Mall, visit and browse through baby stores, and buy something for our baby."

"That's an excellent idea," Jim said, looking at his watch.

"It's only 12 o'clock. Why don't you leave around 4 o'clock, do some shopping, then we can meet for dinner. As you leave the shopping center parking lot, at the light, turn right going west. In about less than a mile to your right, there is a nice restaurant, the Red Pheasant. See you there around 6:30. I love you, bye."

"I love you, too, see you later, bye-bye."

As soon as Jennifer hung up went to the bathroom to take a shower.

I am going to look my best this evening, she thought, *and make Jim so proud of me. He is going to have two angels now, a big one, and a small one.*

Jennifer opened the shower door, turned the water on, and got undressed. She checked the water with her hand, and when it was comfortable, she got in and closed the door. As the water was running down, through the steamed glass, you could see Jennifer's smiling face framed by the wet locks of her brown hair. She looked radiant and happy, like a child, after getting the biggest and the best Christmas present ever.

Jim was beside himself with happiness in his office. After he hung up, took Jennifer's picture from his desk, and held it against his heart for awhile. Then he brought the picture to his lips and kissed the warm glass several times.

It was about 4 o'clock and Jennifer had just finished getting dressed ready to drive to Plaza Mall.

Her appearance this afternoon projected a blend of coquettish femininity with a touch of innocent playful sensuality.

Jennifer had on Jim's favorite outfit, the one he found and bought for her at Harrods' the last time he was in London.

It was a two piece fine tweed fall suit dress; a mixture of brown and clay color. The fitted jacket, four inches below the waist long and buttoned up in front, reached a clay color silk scarf around Jennifer's neck. The skirt, medium-short length, was accented with suede leather at the hem to match the bottom of jacket. All leather accessories were the same, including a cute hat with a clay color ribbon. Jennifer's friends were envious, and admired the uncanny taste Jim had in choosing clothes, that made her look so stylish and elegant.

It was 5:45 when Jim left the office.

He figured out coming from east, and away from the busy westbound traffic, needed only thirty minutes to get to the restaurant. When he arrived, he was able to make a left turn into the parking lot right away. He was surprised that there was no westbound traffic at all.

The parking lot attendant opened the door; Jim got out of the car and asked him,

"What is going on? There is no traffic coming from the mall. That's very unusual. This is a heavy traffic time."

"Sir, there has been an accident. It happened ten minutes ago, at the exit of the mall. A policeman just drove by said the westbound exit was closed, and that there were many cars backed up in the Mall parking lot."

"I was to meet my wife here for dinner at 6:30. She is probably stuck. I am going back to look for her."

"Sir, the best way to reach the westbound exit from here, turn right from the parking lot, then right again at the first light. In about five hundred feet to your right, you will see the entrance sign. After you are in, stay straight. You will see the westbound exit to your right."

"Thank you very much for you help."

Jim tipped the attendant, got in the car and drove away. Once at the Mall, he easily found the westbound exit.

There were at least one hundred cars waiting to get through. Jim thought that the best way to find Jennifer was to park his car and walk down to the exit alongside the cars.

He parked his car and started walking fast. After he past at least fifty cars, there was no sight of Jennifer's. He accelerated his pace, and all of a sudden he could see the traffic light, flashing red, police cars, an ambulance, and a fire truck. Jim, very concerned, started running fast along the last cars, until he reached the exit. He looked to his right and saw Jennifer's car. It was halfway on the sidewalk, wedged between a utility pole and a city truck.

Jim became extremely tense, instantly run towards Jennifer's car, but was stopped by a policeman. Jim started fighting and screamed at the top of his lungs,

"This is my wife's car, is she all right? Let me go. I want to see her. Please take me to her. Oh God, I hope she's not hurt."

While Jim was held back by the policeman, the fire squad used an ax and a tire iron forcefully opened the right front door. Access from the driver's door was not possible. The door was pushed in, and was still blocked by the truck. Once the right front door was opened, the lifeless body of Jennifer was seen slumped over to the right, on top of a Teddy bear and a fluffy baby blanket. On the floor, in front of the passenger's seat, Jennifer's purse was visible.

A police captain, carrying Jennifer's purse, approached

Jim, who was still very anxious and distraught, and showed him the purse.

"Sir, do you recognize the name on the credit card, and the signature on the receipt? There were inside this purse."

"Yes, it's my wife's - Jennifer Woodman. Please, let me see her, please oh God please, I hope she is not hurt," Jim answered in a trembling voice.

A second policeman came by and held Jim by the other arm, as Jennifer's body was carried on a stretcher to the ambulance, to be transported to the coroner's office.

With two policemen holding Jim, the police captain placed his right arm on Jim's left shoulder, and with a sympathetic and soft voice said,

"Mr. Woodman, about thirty minutes ago, a terrible accident happened. A city truck driver failed to yield, didn't even slow down according to two witnesses, while making a left turn, and hit your wife's car very hard. I am sorry your wife sustained massive injuries and pronounced dead at the scene."

Jim collapsed and was carried by the two policemen to the sidewalk. He sat by the curb, covered his face with his hands, sobbed uncontrollably and cried out,

"Oh my God, Jennifer is dead. Oh my God my beautiful Jennifer and our baby are gone. Yes, both are gone. How can it be possible? Just six hours ago, we had the time of our life. I cannot believe it. Both of my angels are gone. Oh, God help me."

The policemen helped Jim to the back seat of the captain's car. One policeman stayed with him, closed the door, and the captain drove away.

If happiness could be measured by height, just six hours ago, Jim and Jennifer touched and ruled the skies. Six hours later, both fell to their death.

Jennifer's natural life ended, and Jim's love life ended. The difference is that the former is final, the latter is not.

The beginning of life is somewhat predictable, the ending never.

A little over a month had gone by since Jennifer's death. In times of tragedy, support from relatives and long time close friends is expected and taken for granted.

Jim was overwhelmed with the support and concern that came out of his office. He was given indefinite time off with full pay and the decision when to come back was left up to him.

Last night, Jim called Karen, his assistant, for the first time and asked her to inform the president that this coming Monday he would be back to work full time.

In passing, Karen mentioned to Jim that the company planned to give him various options to help him put his life back together. One was to work out of the London office for a while.

After the phone call, Jim thought about it and felt it was a good idea. Changes of surroundings and a new environment might sooth emotions and transform despair to curiosity that could uncover different opportunities and directions for a new beginning.

It was late Friday afternoon and everybody had left the office. Jim's first week back to work was extremely busy. Although overworked, he welcomed the opportunity to channel his energy and thoughts to something more positive and away from sadness, emptiness, and emotional suspension.

He tried to reason with the new reality, but the facts remained the same. His life was irrevocably altered by the loss of Jennifer and the child both had hoped for.

Jim's unanswered question, consciously and subconsciously, was how anyone transitions from the reality of a life built on invincible rock, anticipated exuberance, emotional comfort, and unrestrained familiarity to the unknown, unpredictability, uncertainty, and to the alluring and fleeting promise of future happiness. The uniqueness of the past experience, with the capture of an unprecedented and almost unattainable depth of joy and communion could be a handicap in assessing emergence of new dreams and emotions. Attachment to the past could blind one's vision to see not a better, but a different kind of brilliance.

Jim gladly accepted the London position, and planned to move in about six weeks. The company maintained for its executives and guests a luxurious furnished suite of four separate sleeping quarters, with their sitting and workstation areas. A large living room and a fully equipped kitchen was accessible and available to all guests. Four floors below was the company's business office, where all transactions were conducted. This arrangement eliminated travel time, although a company car was available.

It was 7:30 in the evening, and Jim was still in the office, taking a second look at the draft proposals he planned to present to the board of directors next week concerning the London operations. He was ready to call it a day.

As he turned around to pick up his briefcase from the credenza, stared at Jennifer's picture for sometime, picked it up, kissed it, and put it back. A note was taped on his briefcase. 'Mr. W, your appointment with Ms. Hofmeister is on Monday at 9:30. I was told to cancel all your meetings for the entire day. Have a nice weekend. See you on Tuesday, Karen.'

When Jim returned to work on Monday he met with Steve, the company president. He mentioned the attorney's name. The managing partner of the law firm that represented the company was a close friend of Steve's. He highly recommended Erica Hofmeister, a brilliant attorney, and a star of the firm's trial team. Jim knew and understood that legal proceedings were necessary but he wasn't looking forward to dealing with them. The driver of the city truck had pleaded guilty to vehicular homicide and was awaiting sentencing. Jennifer's life insurance provided by her employer, which had a double indemnity clause in case of accidental death, would be paid to him very soon with no hassle. The only thing he needed now was serenity, internal reconciliation, hope, closure; not legal briefs, affidavits, and depositions.

The weekend kept Jim very busy and took his mind off Monday's meeting with the attorney. He dreaded reliving and recalling the circumstance surrounding Jennifer's death. He was happy the house was sold, and Good Will Industries and

Salvation Army picked up all Jennifer's stuff, her clothes, car, and all the furniture. He kept only a single bed, he had already moved to his computer room, where he slept after Jennifer's death.

He couldn't wait to leave the house. He made arrangements to move to a hotel close to his office the following week to stay, until he was ready to move to London.

Monday morning, around 8:50, Jim dressed impeccably as usual was ready to go. After having a cup of black coffee, he never was a breakfast person, left for the attorney's office. He parked his car and went to the main lobby to check the directory. Erica Hofmeister's office was located on the eleventh floor. Jim took the elevator, and when it stopped and the door opened, he walked directly into the law firm's reception lobby. It was large, expensively and tastefully decorated but not overbearing. The name of the law firm, MOYAR, MOYAR & ASSOCIATES, PA was imposingly displayed above the receptionist's desk.

Jim approached the receptionist and introduced himself.

"Good morning Miss. My name is James Woodman. I have a 9:30 appointment with Ms. Hofmeister."

"Good morning Mr. Woodman, I am very sorry, Ms. Hofmeister, on her way to the office was called for an emergency meeting at another attorney's office. Please, accept her apologies. She will be thirty to forty minutes late. I will take you to her office now. Would like a cup of coffee?"

"No, thanks."

The receptionist got up, started walking, and Jim followed her. She turned left to a large arched hallway that looked more like a gallery. Impressive tapestry was on the walls, which were covered with portraits of distinguish looking ladies and gentlemen.

The receptionist, an impressive brunette in her twenties, dressed out of Vogue magazine, with the walk and the moves of a supper model but more intelligent and animated, turned into Erica's office.

"Mr. Woodman, please have a seat, and make yourself comfortable. If you need anything, please let me know," the receptionist said and walked out.

Jim picked up a copy of Forbes magazine, and started reading.

Erica's office was furnished in grandeur manner, as expected from a law firm with national and international clientele; expensive, and somewhat austere, but not intimidating. It was large enough to accommodate a green leather-tufted sofa, and three matching chairs; two armchairs, and a desk chair. There was a large oval table in front of the sofa, with many magazines and newspapers spread on the glass top. Erica's desk was curved in front, and made of mahogany like the rest of the furniture. The walls were paneled in oak, like the parquet wood flooring. Three oriental rugs of geometrical design and mixed colors were scattered throughout the room. On the wall, behind the desk chair, Erica's diplomas were hung.

In the left corner, there was a magnificent chess set of intricately carved out of ivory figures, sitting on a full-size chessboard and table combination. The lighting, coming from recessed fixtures in the ceiling and a desk lamp, was soft.

Jim put the magazine down and glanced around. He noticed that there weren't any family pictures. He vividly remembered the feeling of joy, longing, connection, and anticipation he always experienced when looking at Jennifer's picture. After Jennifer's death the picture was still there, but the feelings had changed to dreams to be lived only in Utopia. Jim picked up the Wall Street Journal now, and went back to his reading.

Erica Hofmeister, Jim's attorney to be, a person with unusual character and personality, was very complex. Every part of her was so unique, that the combination made her formidable. Erica's father, a hard driven executive in banking and commercial real estate development, died from a massive heart attack at the age of forty-eight. Her mother, a beautiful woman, died from acute leukemia at the age of forty, two years later, when Erica was ten years old. A large trust fund and property left to Erica made her wealthy at that young age.

Erica, after her mother's death, moved in to live with her single aunt Mary, her mother's older sister and only sibling. Her father was an only child. Aunt Mary was an extremely intelligent and educated woman, with a Ph.D. in child development from Columbia University Teacher's College. She was the headmistress of a very competitive private school for girls that Erica had attended.

Erica was a precocious child who taught herself to read before she was three.

As Erica grew older, it became obvious that she inherited her mother's arresting looks, combined with the aggressive ambition, analytical mind, determination, and confidence of her father's. All these qualities were nurtured by her aunt Mary, who became her intellectual soul mate. She died two years ago, and Erica missed her a lot.

Erica's academic performance, especially in her senior year in high school, broke all the charts, and although the combination of looks and brains were intimidating to others, left her unaffected. She dressed simply but elegantly, wearing very little makeup or none at all, and seldom any jewelry. This made her beauty more natural and enigmatic. Socially Erica was friendly, but reserve, and her dating was very selective, sporadic, and mostly functionary, like attending school dances.

Erica graduated at the top of her class, and her valedictorian address ended with; "If you want to succeed in life, like in school, always do your home work, be prepared, know you competitors, have alternate plans, make no excuses, and be ready to start over."

Erica was voted 'Not the most likely to succeed but to conquer.' Below her picture in the yearbook of the graduating class were two entries written by a student that actually depicted how her classmates perceived Erica; 'Ice Queen' and 'Ms. Brain.'

Erica attended and excelled at Harvard, and became the leading member of the debating team.

Aunt Mary agreed with her advisor that with her skills and physical presence, she was borne to be a lawyer. Erica was accepted to several Ivy League law schools, including Harvard, but she chose the University of Chicago. She liked the insular and contemplative neutrality of the Midwest; rich in academia and culture, with no self-serving claim to sophistication that was so common in the East.

She was appalled, during Commencement Exercises at Harvard, that some graduates came to receive their diplomas in flip flops or gym shoes, wearing T-shirts and old frayed denim shorts under their gowns. Erica thought, *This was the most exaggerated form of snobbery to conceal deeply seeded subconscious insecurity.* In Erica's opinion, there were other ways to blaze the trail, without demeaning one's self or exhibiting barbaric and vulgar behavior, just to prove that they were different, and liberated from conventionality. Erica's comments and opinions could be funny, serious, caustic, incisive, allegorical, many a time expressed in uncanny metaphors. Erica had been with the same law firm since graduation and had earned the admiration and respect not only of her colleagues but her competitors as well.

Socially as an attorney, Erica was properly pleasant, but eclectic and remote, exhibiting the same unintentional aloofness she was known for. She was totally committed to her profession, and marriage might be an unexpected eventuality in the future, but the thought was very distant and undefined. Erica analyzed, calculated, and articulated her objectives carefully and logically. Then, methodically devised strategies and set priorities in order to win.

Her presence could be overwhelming. She was five feet eight inches tall in her early thirties. She had big green eyes, and her ears, nose, lips, cheekbones, and chin were in perfect architectural harmony with each other. Her natural auburn hair, parted in the middle, reached the lower part of her neck. Today, her finely proportioned silhouette was draped in a light gray, two piece custom-made Armani suit, the hemline of the skirt right at the knee, a white blouse, and comfortable two inches heel brown pumps. Erica wore expensive and fashionable clothes, but when it came to the hemline of skirts and dresses for business attire the strategy was defense.

She always kept in her mind the same picture, and recalled it with amusement- the contortions and the twisting gyrations some 'fashionable' professional women wearing shorts skirts or dresses go through in order to avoid collateral exposure, while trying to sit down. To prevent accidents, fast crossing of the legs is the strategy, but the time allowed-measured in nanoseconds-makes the effort rarely attainable, even for women with Amazonian skills. And once they sit down, the pull and tug phase begins.

Erica's makeup was light, and she wore no jewelry except for her gold Rolex watch. She always maintained eye contact with her clients, and spoke in a soft feminine and reassuring voice, never losing her professional demeanor and authority.

Jim's reading was suddenly interrupted. A hidden door, from the right wooden paneled wall opened, and Erica walked in. Jim got up, walked to her, shook hands, exchanged pleasantries and both sat on the sofa.

"Mr. Woodman, I apologize for being late. On my way to the office, my cell phone rang, and I was asked to attend a rather urgent meeting at another attorney's office. I appreciate your taking the day off from your busy schedule, but it is important that we meet, get acquainted, and get familiarized with what lies ahead; the strategy and process involved.

Mr. Woodman, I am very sorry for the loss of your wife and unborn child. There is nothing that can be done to bring them back to life, or replace them. I hope, with the passage of time you will find solace and reconcile the past with the present. The insurance for the city accepted total liability for the accident, and proposed to settle out of court. The dollar figure offered, for some may be reasonable, but for me was unacceptable. If you are thinking of settling the case, I am sorry I will withdraw from representing you, and as far as I know no other attorney from this firm will agree to take the case."

Erica got up, took a few steps, leaned on the edge of

her desk and placed both hands on top, stared at Jim, and continued;

"Mr. Woodman, two lives were lost. Pain and suffering has become your constant companion. There isn't enough of anything in the entire world that could compensate you for your loss. It is my responsibility, as your attorney, to make sure that your compensation measures up, if this is possible, to what you have been deprived of, no more and no less. A jury in a court of law should hear and determine the value of two lives lost, whose opportunities to reach their potential as members of a loving family, and productive members of society were untimely and abruptly interrupted."

While Erica was speaking, Jim kept his head down, and continued for a minute or two in complete silence after she finished, wondering, *Is Erica a compassionate human being or a cold hearted, deliberate, and expedient attorney tying to build up the focus of her legal strategy?*

Jim raised his head, and looked Erica in the eyes.

"Ms. Hofmeister, we are practically strangers. We met less than ten minutes ago, and in no uncertain terms, you clearly articulated what is deeply buried in my heart and mind, but seldom externalized by me or acknowledged by others."

Jim stopped for a few seconds, regained his composure and continued,

"Ms. Hofmeister, I really appreciate the concern and interest you have in my case, but you have to understand how I feel. Jennifer was my life, and the child, our child that she was carrying was going to be the crown in our state of happiness. There is no money, irrespective of the amount, that is going to change what I feel and bring back what I have lost. Playing to the emotions of the jury is not only unbecoming to my feelings, but to Jennifer's memory as well. I have found some solace and tranquility lately by being more private, and emotionally self-contained. To express and expose my feelings in an open courtroom, will totally deconstruct and derail my present state of mind. Healing and acceptance of the events that led to the greatest loss of my life would be interrupted, and pain would resurface with new intensity."

There was silence in the office.

Erica sat down on the armchair to the right of Jim and became pensive. She understood well Jim's present state of mind, kept quiet, and started thinking, *The way Jim was talking about a woman, wife or not, was totally strange to her. She knew that falling in love was a human condition, mostly celebrated in romantic novels and the cinema. She never realized the depth and the power love could reach in real life that could transform two individuals into a single entity that made their interdependence secure and happy.* Erica believed that mature and developed people like herself in order to function, by exercising their mental skills and applying their intellectual powers to the fullest, are always able to be in total control of emotions and psyche. Erica felt that if love was such a compelling force, that completely eliminated all boundaries of individuality, and possibly compromised one's independence was not for her. Or love could be something of a fair exchange. Maybe by loving and giving part of yourself, you could discover another dimension of a different power, which without love would have never been tapped, or even worse, totally wasted.

Erica got off the chair, went back and sat on the sofa next to Jim.

"Mr. Woodman, in planning my legal strategy, I always respect the feelings, emotions, and the privacy of my clients. I have already thought out alternatives that would be responsive and sensitive to your frame of mind and needs, without compromising serious legal venues, that as your attorney, I have to pursue. Let me outline what my plans and strategy are in trying this case.

To begin with, the suit requesting a jury trial will be filed no matter what the offer to settle is. The insurance company will understand how serious we are. In my experience, when liability has been admitted, even while the case is being tried, settlement is highly possible, but on our own terms. Any smart attorney would do his or her best to avoid a jury judgment where the level of emotion and personal experience count. You need only one juror, who had a friend of a friend involved in such a tragedy and the jury's decision can be devastating. In case your testimony is needed, so that the jury, first hand, can value your loss, we can have your sworn deposition videotaped and played in court. As you see, with this arrangement, the entire process would be simplified, requiring very little of your time, and the very minimal, but necessary participation from you."

"Ms. Hofmeister, I listened very carefully to everything you said. I am trying to logically and emotionally justify and accept your strong opinions and recommendations, while I maintain my own personal level of comfort. I know you were highly recommended as a dedicated professional, who uses her expertise to the fullest committed to get the best outcome for your clients.

People face different predicaments in their lifetime, and dealing with them and the individuals who try to help them can be very taxing. I strongly believe that in addition to professional competence, a certain degree of trust is important. I have to trust your judgment. You can go ahead with your legal plans and try this case in court if you see certain merit to it. What moved me in this direction was your thoughtfulness and sensitivity to find a way to shelter my privacy and protect my present state of mind in planning and initiating the necessary legal proceedings."

"Mr. Woodman, I value your trust as you expressed it. It will give me an additional gear in my effort and strategy to overcome future eventualities in this case. I would like you to be aware, that at this time, this is the only court case I have been assigned to. This will allow me to devote all my time and energy in preparing and trying this case.

Three weeks ago, I was informed of my transfer from the trial to the corporate division of the firm. This is a big career opportunity with new challenges and responsibilities for me that will require a great deal of traveling. I have been told that in a few weeks you will be moving to the London office of your company, responsible for the European operations. Last year, I did some work for your company in London and stayed at the suite above the main office. The apartment was nice, in a good location, and close to shopping and entertainment sites."

Erica and Jim got up and shook hands.

"Mr. Woodman, it was nice to have met you. The receptionist will give you my business card with my home phone number written on. When you move to London, because of the time difference, don't hesitate to call me at home if you have any questions. How long will it take to close your case is impossible to predict. It may take a few months or years. Goodbye, and have a nice trip. We'll keep in touch."

"Ms. Hofmeister, thanks for everything. It was nice meeting you, too. Goodbye."

Jim, on his way out, stopped by the receptionist's desk to pick up Erica's business card.

Erica after Jim left, and being analytical by nature, wondered what the future would hold for a person like him. *Would he ever be free to redirect his emotions, love again, seek the warmth and comfort of another woman? Could she prevail or would she be a substitute for companionship, happiness, and love lost? The relationship and the emotional attachment of Jim to Jennifer,* Erica thought, *were still very strong and overpowering despite the absence of the ability to physically communicate. It was obvious, that in Jim's heart and mind, Jennifer's presence was very much alive. Could it be possible that destiny and fate would unlock the door to a different future and level of existence for Jim, that would not replace his wondrous experience of the past, but present him with new opportunities to explore unfamiliar territories that may surprise him with a different dimensions of happiness?*

Jim, after left Erica's office, as he was driving home, tried to assess her. Jim believed that it was not only natural, but also important to be curious and inquisitive about people you trust to take care of serious and personal matters. He had so many questions.

Erica's appearance was astonishing, and her intelligence, language, confidence, and professionalism could evoke admiration, envy, and even fear. Jim thought, *What could a woman, like Erica, so perfect on the outside, possess inwardly as a human being? Could she feel pain, understand someone's sorrow or joy? Accept and give love? Laugh, or cry? Be vulnerable and playful? Or could her physical appearance and beauty, combined with strong mental and intellectual gifts, and framed by an aloof and controlled persona, be barriers to the discovery of human emotions, feelings, and sentiments?* The question that constantly preoccupied Jim's mind was, *Has Erica, as an individual with all her gifts and composite brilliance, both intellectual and physical, achieved integration of mind and heart to become whole as human being, in the classical concept of proportional perfection? She talks the talk for sure. Can she walk the walk, too?*

CHAPTER TWO

RECONSTRUCTION

Jim worked in London close to three years. As a bright man with depth, if he had to precisely define this part of his life, he would call it the period of 'reconstruction.'

When adversity unexpectedly strikes and disrupts the delicate balance between the mind and the heart, the consequences can be devastating. People with strong minds like Jim understand the aching of the heart and through time and reason, try to rebuild the bridge of balanced happiness between them. When the heart becomes weaker, the mind becomes stronger and fills in. When minds and hearts are integrated, emotional vacuums are not allowed. Slowly thinking and feeling become equally strong again; supporting, understanding, guiding and celebrating each other.

Jim, as head of European operations, accomplished a great deal since coming to London and the growth of all accounts exceeded all predictions. Two weeks ago, Steve Larson, the president of the company, sent Jim a congratulatory memo praising him for his performance. The memo was also distributed to board of directors, and posted in the employees' lounge. It was obvious that Jim's promotion to vice president was certain when his overseas assignment was over. Jim had mixed emotions, but was looking forward to going back to U.S.

His professional growth and success, along with the anticipated promotion gave him a great sense of pride, but at the same time made him melancholic. There was no one back home close to him to share his happiness and be a loving and supportive partner to his expanding and successful career. Celebrating success alone tarnishes its luster. It's like eating an elaborate, exquisite, carefully prepared, and fancily served dinner alone - tasteful and glamorous, but boring! Jennifer's memory remained vivid in Jim's mind and heart. He started to realize it was possible that another woman could come along not as a replacement or substitute, but a woman with her own qualities. One capable of opening a new chapter in his life journey. Jim's desire to become a father remained very strong, but he would never consider remarrying just to have a child, compromising his many positive emotional experiences of the past.

While in London, Jim never dated or actively sought female companionship, although many opportunities came along. He remained rather neutral, and all his contacts with women were either professional or socially dictated by business and office etiquette.

Jim's work was his only objective at this time of his life. His hard work and dedication explained his high productivity. The company was so sympathetic and understanding during his personal tragedy, he was happy to be able to give something back in return. Being alone, he felt neither lonely nor unhappy. He thought of his past with some degree of sadness, but treasured all the good memories that nothing and nobody could take them from him.

Happiness interrupted is not happiness lost, unless built on lies and deception. It's like an old photograph of someone very dear. Stains and fading would never diminish its value. Jim believed he was blessed to have found love of such depth that after the initial despair gave him the strength to live, love life, and be whole again, with mind and heart united.

The last time Jim heard from Erica Hofmeister, his attorney, was six months ago, after his videotaped testimony was reviewed by the defense and the actuary staff of the insurance company. She said the impact was tremendous, and the offer to settle out of court was upped, but rejected. She gave them another six months extension with the understanding that if settlement could not be reached during this period of time the case would go to trial.

It was 6:30 in the morning in London.

Jim just finished making corrections, and added new entries on the monthly report due to be e-mailed to U.S. Headquarters next week. He liked to start working early and enjoyed being alone in the office. Suddenly, the phone interrupted the silence and Jim answered.

"This is Jim Woodman, London office, may I help you?"

"Hi Jim, how are you? Can you tell who is calling?"

"I have a hunch, but I am not sure."

"This is Erica, your attorney from U.S."

"Oh my goodness, I suspected it, but I wasn't sure. Do you know what threw me off?"

"What," Erica asked.

"You called me by my first name, Jim, for the first time. If you don't mind, I will call you Erica."

"By all means do. I am so excited! The insurance company agreed to everything we asked and a letter of intent to settle out of court has been signed by all principals."

"That's fantastic Erica. I don't have to appear in court. You promised me that the first time we met, and you carried through. I will always be grateful to you for that. By the way, what are you doing up so late. What time is it?"

"It's past midnight. I didn't want to wait until tomorrow to give you the good news. Besides, because of the time difference, one of us has to be up late. Next time is your turn."

"What happened? When did you meet with the attorney for the insurance company?" Jim asked.

"When I had my last meeting with Tracy Butler, I was prepared to be more frank than aggressive, and articulate your feelings as honestly as I could, and said that he couldn't imagine the impact that Jennifer's death had upon you. You and your wife dreamed of having a baby, and together went through pain, both physical and emotional and had finally succeeded. You not only lost your life long companion and love, but the opportunity to hold, kiss, caress, and sing to your baby.

At this point, Butler requested to be alone in our teleconference room, to consult with the insurance company, the actuaries, and his senior partner.

Butler and I never were legal adversaries in the past, but we knew each other by reputation. Butler is in his mid-fifties, dignified looking, impeccably dressed, and the persona of the upper crust legal presence. He is thin, about six feet tall, handsome and charming, has the mannerism of a diplomat and the piercing eyes of a hawk."

"I am having a good time. Please, tell me more."

"By now you know a little about me. When I negotiate, I don't let anybody intimidate me. I can face the most skillful adversary, man or woman, and make them very careful of what they say and how they respond. Butler understood from the very beginning of our meeting that charm, flattery, or patronizing not only wouldn't work with me, but could diminish his effectiveness. Jim, I never allow my adversaries, no matter how powerful, to constrain my ability to follow through with my legal strategy. Their aggressiveness stimulates me, and enhances my performance. By quick thinking and redirecting my approach, I come up with new arguments that not only surprise and disarm, but even confuse them."

"Oh Erica, I am glad you are on my side. I can imagine how commanding your presence was. Then what happened?"

"Butler was on the phone with his people for close to three hours. When we met again, he said the decision would be made in about three weeks. I reaffirmed our position that all our terms had be accepted in order to settle out of court. Three weeks later, which was today, their office courier brought the letter of intent to my office. I will get back to you when everything has been finalized."

"I would like to thank you for all your efforts. I will be waiting to hear from you. Goodnight."

"I will call you soon. Bye-bye."

After the phone call, Jim was happy and relieved that the case was finally settled. He didn't care to ask the dollar amount involved. Money was the least of his problems at this time of his life. All the proceeds from Jennifer's life insurance and the sale of the house were deposited and left in the U.S. Jim, with his pending return to U.S., had other more pressing issues to consider.

He left the office, took the elevator down to the main floor and decided to take a morning walk, to think and contemplate his future.

Jim was close to celebrating his thirty-eight birthday.

He was a successful executive, educated, sophisticated, sensitive, and sensible man. His desire to have a child remained as strong as ever. The question was how he would find a woman of substance. He detested the contemporary 'singles' life style and the trial and error method looking for a mate. For sure, there would be many women who would like to marry Jim at the drop of the hat. He was a good catch. So he was told. He knew and understood that statistically he couldn't replicate the past. Could the past be a handicap for Jim's future? If he was to lower his expectations, how low was low? Jim, deep in his heart, knew what he wanted. If what Jim wanted was not attainable, would he be better off to look for what he needed?

The answer wasn't easy. Jim still had many questions in his mind but felt positive and relaxed.

The difference of what one wants and what one needs can be very profound.

Jim finished reading The London Times. As he put the paper down looked at his watch. It was 11 o'clock. The last time Jim talked Erica was three weeks ago.

Before he left the office today, he received a fax from Erica to let him know that she would call him at his apartment later in the evening to give him the latest news concerning the settlement.

Jim went to the kitchen to get a glass of water. On his way

back to the living room the phone rang. Jim put the glass down on the coffee table and sat on the sofa close to the side table where the phone was, and answered.

"Hello, Jim speaking."

"Hi Jim, Erica calling, how have you been?"

"I am fine, thank you, what's new?"

"Well, I have good news for you. All the work is done and all affidavits and other legal papers have been signed. To go over the details on the phone is not possible.

I don't know if you remember that this was my last court case before being transferred to the corporate division. The law firm wants me to come to the London office of your company to review some pending legal issues you have. When I come, we can go over the details of the settlement, and answer all of your questions."

"I can't believe it; what a coincidence. I was expecting an attorney from your firm, but even in my wildest imagination, I didn't expect to be you. You are welcome to stay at the company's apartment. You stayed here before and you liked it. Right now, I am the only occupant, and I have a company car at my disposal. Fax me your itinerary. I can pick you up at the airport. What do you say, Erica?"

"That's very nice of you, but I don't want to spoil your routine or be in your way."

"That's silly Erica, you've been here before. There are three empty bedrooms just sitting here. I won't take no for an answer. You worked so hard on my case. Please, give me the opportunity to express my gratitude and be your host. You would be a visitor in London, but at least for the time being, I am still a resident. By the way, three days ago, I was informed that I was promoted to vice president. Now, I am trying to tie up some loose ends and I hope to be back in the States in about two months. The timing of your visit is perfect. We can clear up some important issues, and make it easier for my replacement."

"Congratulations Jim, that's fantastic news! What a coincidence. Since we met, we both got a big boost in our careers; you as vice president of finance, and I as a high profile corporate attorney. We are both accomplished professionals, have arrived, and there is nothing that will ever stand in the way to be even more successful. Thanks for your kind invitation. I am sure you will be a fine host. Goodnight Jim, see you soon."

"Bye-bye Erica, and don't forget to fax me your itinerary."

Jim whenever met and talked to people, reflexively internalized opinions and characterizations to describe them, intended only to be part of his domain and not verbalized. The epithets were descriptive and pertinent to specific instances that fitted perfectly without discrediting other qualities individuals might possess.

Jim, by nature, character, and demeanor, never used four letter or other insulting words. They never became part of his active vocabulary. Tonight, regretfully so, Jim couldn't contain himself. There was a perfect fit.

After he hung-up, Erica's last statement that there was nothing that would stand in their way (meaning in Erica's way) to being even more successful overtook him. It constantly resonated with a deafening and a painful high pitch sound that made Jim lose control. *What an arrogant, controlling, and ambitious bitch with a capital B, Erica is. A lioness never satiated and ready to devour her next prey. No humility*, Jim thought.

The following day Jim received a fax in the office with Erica's itinerary.

She was coming to London next Saturday, staying for a week, and flying back to U.S. the following Saturday. Erica's flight was scheduled to arrive at 10:00 in the morning.

To park at the airport on Saturdays was very difficult with so many domestic and international flights arriving and departing. Parking would be available far away from the terminal that made it inconvenient. Jim thought riding a cab both ways would be much more practical and quicker.

After he got out of the taxi, Jim went directly to the luggage claim area. A flashing light above the carousel showed flight # 611 had just landed. Jim looked at his watch; it was 10 o'clock. Erica's plane was on time.

He started walking towards the escalator that brought passengers to the lower level to pick up their luggage. Jim hadn't seen Erica since he left the U.S., where they met only once in her office, but talked on the phone several times.

A woman with Erica's face, beauty, and grace is never forgotten. Jim was sure he would recognize her right way. They weren't only her physical characteristics and their symmetry, but the mystery she projected. What she concealed was more alluring and mysterious than what she showed.

In a few seconds, Jim saw Erica getting off of the escalator. She smiled. Both walked to each other and exchanged a firm handshake.

"Hi Erica. Welcome to London, nice to see you again. You look fantastic and well rested. Apparently flying over the Atlantic doesn't affect you. You must have a secret for jet lag."

"Jim you look great yourself; more relaxed and less preoccupied. Flying nowadays is more accommodating, and with the seat changing to almost like a bed, you can catnap on and off. Jim thanks again for your invitation and I hope you follow your routine. Please change nothing on my account."

"Don't worry Erica. It is my pleasure to have you as my guest. After we pickup your suitcases, we will get a taxi back to the apartment. It's much easier. How many pieces of luggage you have?"

"Only one. I have my carry-on and my purse with me."

Pretty soon, Erica saw her suitcase coming. She pointed it out to Jim, he picked it up, and they walked out to the sidewalk to get a taxi. The attendant by the 'Taxi' sign whistled and a cab came right away. It stopped where Jim and Erica were standing. The driver got out of the cab and put the suitcases in the trunk. Erica and Jim took the back seat.

With all seated in the cab, the driver asked,

"Where to, Sir?"

"Commerce and Financial Towers, please."

As soon as the taxi started moving, Jim turned his head to Erica and asked,

"After you unpack, would you like something to eat? There are many good restaurants we can walk to or have something at the apartment. As a bachelor, I have developed some cooking skills. I dislike having all my meals out. For dinner we can go out."

"Thanks, Jim. Right now, I am not hungry. What I'd like to do is take a bath, clean up, then sleep for awhile. I still need three to four hours of sleep to become more functional. After my nap and around tea time, as the English are accustomed to, I would like to sit down and explain to you in detail the settlement and its implications. As for dinner, I'd rather stay home tonight. We can do it another day, we have a whole week. I will be flying back to the States next Saturday."

"That's fine with me Erica. We are almost here. Please slow down," Jim said to the cab driver.

The taxi stopped. The driver got out, opened the door, and Jim and Erica got out of the back seat. He picked up the suitcase and the carry-on from the trunk, carried them through the main entrance and placed them by the elevator door, as Jim and Erica walked behind him. As soon as Jim took his wallet out of his pocket to pay the driver, Erica grabbed his hand and stopped him.

"Jim, I am sorry, this is my responsibility and I insist."

She paid the driver, entered the elevator, and while holding the door open, Jim carried inside her suitcase and the carry-on bag.

"I hope we won't have any arguments during my staying in London," Erica said to Jim, smiling.

"I came for serious business but I plan to have a good time and relax, too"

"Erica, I promise. I won't do that again. I plan to have good time, also," Jim said, as the elevator started moving.

When the elevator stopped and the door opened, Erica got out. Jim picked up and carried the luggage, as both walked to the apartment door. Jim put the luggage down, took the key out his pocket, unlocked the door and let Erica in. As she walked inside, Jim carried the luggage and closed the door.

"Jim, the living room is different, since the last time I was here. There is more furniture."

"You are absolutely correct. Since I seldom eat out, the company provided me with a dining room set to compliment the full kitchen. Do you have any preference for the bedroom? They are all the same."

"No, Jim, I know there are all alike."

Jim opened one of the doors from the large living area leading to the bedroom, carried the suitcase and the carry-on bag inside, and put them on top of the bed, as Erica looked around.

"That's very nice. I love the combination of sitting and workstation space. I think I will do most of my work from here, since there is e-mail and a fax machine available. I like the privacy and not having to get dressed up for business every day. I can stop downstairs at the company's office and pick up all the files I need."

"That's fine, Erica. I have separated all the files in question. Oh, by the way, before I forget. The company has added dry cleaning service besides laundry. Just put your stuff in the plastic bag marked for dry cleaning. The service that cleans the bedrooms will take care of it. This apartment idea has saved our company a great deal of money. It was so expensive to maintained hotel suites. And our main office is four floors down." Then Jim, looking at his watch, asked Erica,

"It's 11:30. What time would you like me to wake you up?"

"Don't worry. I will set my alarm clock and meet you at 5 o'clock. I will unpack now, and set your file aside before I do anything else. If it's convenient, when we meet, I would like some fresh fruit and black coffee, if available."

"No problem. My refrigerator is well stocked. Have a nice rest, and I will see you at 5 o'clock. Welcome to London, Erica."

At 5 o'clock exactly, the door from Erica's bedroom to the living room opened.

Erica walked in holding a thick brown file folder and placed it on the dining room table. She looked relaxed and fresh, with no make up visible.

She wore a bright yellow cashmere sweater, light brown Channel woolen slacks, with matching open sandals. Her toenails, with a fine pedicure, were polished in natural color like her fingernails. Her perfume was delicate, enchanting, and unusually pleasant to the sense, as if gardenia buds covered with early summer drops of cool sunrise dew were hidden in the room.

"Good afternoon, Jim."

Erica sat down on a dining room chair, moving the brown folder closer to her.

"Good afternoon to you, Erica. You look so nice and elegant. You make me feel like a bum in my faded blue jeans and old sports shirt."

"You must have forgotten. I am meeting with a very important client and I have to look professional. Don't you think so?"

"You may think you client is important but he doesn't."

Jim went to the kitchen and brought out a platter with seasonal fresh fruit and a coffeepot with fresh brewed coffee. Earlier he had set the dining room table with silverware, china and napkins. He poured coffee for both and sat down across from her. While were sipping coffee, Erica helped herself to some fruit.

"Jim, aren't you going to have some?"

"No," I am doing fine."

Erica opened the thick folder slowly, looked Jim directly in the eyes and with an expression of satisfaction and accomplishment said,

"As your attorney Jim, I am very happy with the outcome. We could have settled earlier, but for a much lesser amount. Jim, please listen carefully. The statement I am about to read, no matter how brief, depicts and summarizes the core of my strategy."

Mr. James Woodman, as a result of this terrible accident that killed his wife and unborn child, suffered irreparable psychological trauma, pain, suffering, loss of consortium, and the prospect of becoming a father. The award for damages that were inflicted upon Mr. Woodman, must be of value measurable to the loss of his wife and unborn child.

"Jim, there is nothing that is going to bring your family back. This maybe difficult for you to understand, but the compensation that measures the value of your loss would only monetary."

Erica took her water glass to her mouth, drank some, and wiped her lips with a napkin.

Jim lowered his head in silence for a few seconds and with teary eyes asked Erica to continue.

"Jim, let me give you some figures. The city is self-insured up to $1 million and was willing settle right away, but the offer was turned down."

Jim became annoyed, tense, and shook his head.

"Why? What were you looking for, Erica?"

"Jim, hear me out. The city has co-insurance that covers catastrophic cases like this one. Once the city's offer was rejected, we negotiated with them. That's where the big dollars came from. The final figure came to $5 million, the highest ever in the county. I am very proud of my win, Jim."

Jim got up, angry and bewildered, started pacing for a while in silence. His face turned red, then he sat down.

"I know you are proud of your win, but I am ashamed. What good is this money is going to do me? Am I going ever to wake up in the morning next to Jennifer? Never. Am I going ever to wake up in middle of the night by our baby's cry? Never. Am I going ever to be strolling our baby in the park? Never. Am I going ever to buy Jennifer a Mother's Day present? Never. Am I going ever to see our baby open Christmas presents? Never. Erica, I congratulate you on your win, but it does nothing to lessen my pain. To me, this is blood money. It's a curse. I had a hunch this could happen after you explained your legal strategy, but now it is real and my heart and mind are thrown into an abysmal spin. If you don't mind, I would like stop this discussion right now. We can continue tomorrow over breakfast."

"That's fine with me. I understand money is not important to you and you don't need it. I am sure you will think of something positive to do with it. You said this money was a curse. Jim, you are a smart man. Think of something. Turn the curse into a blessing. You have a full deck in your hands and it's up to you to make the right call," Erica said somewhat annoyed.

"I didn't mean to upset you. I am sorry. Let's change the subject. What can I fix for supper?"

"Something simple and light. Can you fix a salad?"

"Sure. I have fresh vegetables, and I can toss them with fresh shrimp, if you like."

" I would. For dressing, I would prefer olive oil mixed with lemon juice."

"No problem. In London, we get high quality extra virgin cold pressed olive oil from Greece and Italy."

Jim pickup the dishes, cleaned the table, and brought in clean china and silverware.

"Can I help, Jim?" Erica asked.

"No, not now. You can help me load the dishwasher after we finish eating."

"That's a good idea. I don't like feeling and being treated like a formal guest."

Jim and Erica spoke casually during dinner, but it was apparent that both were preoccupied, detached, neutral and somewhat tense.

Being together for the first time in an informal and personal setting, created for them a mental mixture of contrasting and opposing feelings; hope and despair, warmth and remoteness, commitment and independence, control and abandon.

Intelligent minds like Jim and Erica's, irrespective of their psyches and personal perceptions, focus and refocus constantly with high velocity. They store images and thoughts from the past and present, then selectively recall and analyze them, and try to find out if and how affected they are by them.

After dinner Jim and Erica, sat quietly in the living room for a while, but it was obvious that both were tired.

"Jim, it's only 9 o'clock, but I am ready to hit the sack. I don't know about you. Thanks for a wonderful dinner and I hope tomorrow over breakfast to finish our discussion concerning the settlement."

"I hope so, too. I don't want this to hang over me for too long."

Jim and Erica got up, said goodnight, walked to their bedrooms, and waved at each other before closing the door.

Erica went through her usual routine before going to bed. She got undressed, put a robe and a pair slippers on, went to the bathroom to brush her teeth and hair, then covered her face with a cleansing cream and wiped it off with facial pads.

She, from early age, was a ferocious reader. No matter where she was, or how tired, or what time, one hour of reading was part also of her routine before going to sleep, never missed as far as she could remembered.

Tonight was different. Erica sat down without a book in her hands, but with a plethora of images, old and new ones, that her mind recalled, compared, sorted out, valued, rejoiced, accepted or rejected.

Erica hadn't slept with a man nearby since her father died. Her aunt Mary never had any male friends for sleepovers or even socially, and her whole life was her work.

Erica had fond memories of her father. She lionized him, and he became the dominant male figure in her life. He loved her very much, and she loved him too, but he was rather restrained in showing physical affection. Both were bright, with quick and uneasy minds, had formed more of an intellectual connection than a sentimental one. They were more like pals, despite the fact that Erica was so young.

One of the highlights was the time her father taught her how to play chess at the age of four. She was fascinated by the different sizes, shapes, movements, and the fact that every chessman had an identical twin, but of a different color. To Erica's mind this became the personification of one's alter ego. Same dynamics, but different circumstances. Her father's chess set in her office became a symbol and a connection to her past, and an allegoric reference Erica used for the rest of her life. Her participation in the last debate at Harvard as a senior was memorable.

The topic was 'Feminism in the last part of the twentieth century.' Her opposing team lamented, 'The inhuman oppression of women through the centuries' and the main premise was, that 'if it weren't for women's liberation movement in the last part of the twentieth century, oppression of women would have continued.'

Erica strongly disagreed. 'Great women,' she argued, 'existed before the women's lib movement, but their accomplishments were deliberately ignored by the hard core feminists. Famous artists, poets, doctors, historians, philosophers, and even Nobel Prize winners, all women, were forgotten in the bra-burning frenzy. The Nobel Prize, the highest award for scientific and literary accomplishments, in its over one hundred years of existence, has been won twice, only once by the same person. And that person was a woman! Marie Curie, 1903 in Physics, and 1911 in Chemistry. Women's liberation movement has become women's libertines movement trying to alter the uniqueness of the Female Psyche, and brainwash and control women with totalitarian and proletarian agendas laced with ultra-liberalism in a highly politicized environment of mass hysteria, that they themselves have created.

Real feminism empowers and compels women to excel. For smart women equality to men may lead to intellectual concession. Real feminism pushes women not to be equal, but better than men by reaching their own potential.

Chess has been played for thousands of years. There are two competing teams with eighteen pieces each. Which piece, in the leadership line of both camps, is the most powerful? The answer is the Queen. The Queen can move to all directions, offensively and defensively, with resolve and power. And what piece, in the leadership line, is the most impotent and weak? The King! The King can make only one limited and pathetic move of one step at a time, just around himself, like a cripple! The King's offensive and defensive capability is zero. The King is a symbol and nothing else. The King relies on the Queen to save his butt and keep him in power. The women's lib movement wants you to become weak and impotent kings. Real feminism wants you to stay powerful and resolute Queens. The choice is obvious.' Erica won the debate.

Erica's social contacts with men were limited. Men thought she was cold and aloof. She was nicknamed 'the untouchable.' She would decline dates for the sake of dating, but would invite single male friends and colleagues to attend opera, symphony, theater, and movies. Whenever Erica invited male companions, she would pay for dinner and tickets. If she liked the company and was invited back, she would let her escort reciprocate.

Erica sensed there was something different tonight that she had never felt before. Was it security, warmth, comfort? Could it be that subconsciously knowing that a man was nearby changed the level of her awareness of feelings that were strange and unfamiliar to her?

Jim, since Jennifer's death close to three years ago, never had a woman guest for dinner or a sleepover in his apartment. He almost forgot how nice and relaxing was to have a woman around, even under these unusual circumstances. He vividly recalled Jennifer's smile, radiant personality, and soothing voice. Erica was so different. The more he knew her, the more curious Jim became. To say the least, she was the most unusual woman he had ever met. Extremely beautiful, bright, cerebral, articulate, determent, elegant, and at the same time blasé and indifferent, making no effort to impress. Jim was wondering, *Was Erica naturally secure or her façade of indifference was intended to make her more conspicuous and be talked about?*

Jim had a hard time falling asleep. His mind and body relentlessly twirled, spun, tossed, and turned to exhaustion.

His mattress felt as if it was filled with sharp stones cutting deep into his flesh and the comforter became a punishing whip that left ugly welts on his skin without mercy. All of a sudden everything stopped. Jim became serene. His face lit up and his smile signaled victory, reconciliation and eternal peace. Soon, Jim fell asleep like a baby, with the taste of fresh warm milk in his mouth, right out of a loving mother's tender breast.

The next day, Jim and Erica had breakfast about 9:30.

"Thanks for a nice breakfast," Erica said. Then she took and moved in front of her, the brown folder left on the dining room table from last night.

"Jim, I know you were upset last night and you didn't want to continue. Have you given any thoughts concerning the settlement? Sooner or later you have to face it, and the sooner the better, no matter how hard and difficult it might be. I hope we can finish it today, so that we can start addressing important issues concerning the office."

Jim took his half filled water glass to his mouth, drank it, put it back on the table, and with a confident and resolute voice replied.

"I couldn't go to sleep last night, even hours after I went to bed. All of a sudden something hit me, hit me really hard, like an explosion, that made me aware of what was deeply buried in my heart and mind, that wanted to come out with a compelling force. It was like an epiphany."

Erica, with her green eyes wide open in astonishment and surprise asked,

"My goodness, your frame of mind and your disposition are so different today. What happened?"

"You're absolutely right, and I will tell why. By now you should know how happy Jennifer and I were. The only thing missing was a child.

Thanks to modern medicine, Jennifer became pregnant through in vitro fertilization, after the third implant. Until then, we had no idea how expensive the procedure could be.

We were fortunate and able, no matter what the cost, to pay ourselves with no hardship. Jennifer and I, during the various phases of the procedure, discussed how disheartening would be for many couples, like ourselves, who would like to have a child, but because of limited means, couldn't afford to go ahead with it. Well Erica, I made my decision and never felt so peaceful in my entire life. I never felt so close to Jennifer and at the same time so free. I could see Jennifer's face smiling at me with love, consent, and pride. What Jennifer and I started, but never came into being, other couples with no means should be given the opportunity to complete and become parents.

The proceeds from the entire settlement, minus legal fees and other expenses, will be donated to the University Fertility Center, as a restricted fund, under the name of 'Jennifer Woodman Foundation.' The generated income should be exclusively used to help infertile married couples to have a child. No good people should be deprived of the opportunity to become parents or the joy of raising and nurturing a child because they are poor."

Erica the Cool, and always in control, was deeply moved. She got up, went around, and placed her hands on Jim's shoulders.

Jim got up; Erica hugged him tight for a second or two, as their faces touched. "I am deeply moved by your generosity, strength, and foresight. It also tells me how much a child meant to you, and what a great man you are. You may be sad but you're not bitter."

Erica went back to her seat, and she and Jim sat down again, across from each other.

"Jim, once the opportunity was given to you, you wanted others to find happiness that eluded you at this time of you life. Jim you're a blessed man, and I hope and wish, sometime in the future, you will live your dreams again under a new, not better but different, perspective."

Jim and Erica, for the first time, appeared to be at ease with each other.

Erica never saw or witnessed love of such depth and

wisdom. It would have been perfectly legal and ethical for Jim to keep all the money for himself. And what did he do? He gave it all away. Not out of guilt, social pressure, ambition, or expediency, but out of the purest and the most selfless love of all loves; the love of sharing with people he would never meet.

"Erica, there is something else I would like tell you. I know financing and investing very well, but I am not an attorney. You are, and a topnotch one. If we combine expertise we can accomplish something great for the foundation. I will be moving back to the States in about two months and visit the London office only for a week, two to three times a year.

When you are back in U.S., visit the CEO of the University Fertility Center and make him aware of my decision. My wish is, and make sure he understands, that you will be appointed the legal counsel of 'Jennifer Woodman Foundation,' responsible for writing the charter of incorporation and all other legal matters. You and another member of your law firm will become members of the Board of Directors of the Foundation."

"That's a great honor. My firm serves in several boards in the community. For me your decision is of particular significance because it will give me the opportunity to follow through with what I have worked so hard for. On a personal basis, I would enjoy seeing you not as your attorney, but as your friend as well. I have great hopes for the foundation you are dedicating to your wife's memory, and I am sure it will help the community in a very positive way."

"You took the words out of my mouth. I met you in the most difficult and devastating time of my life. You worked hard, used your professional skills well, and above all, you kept me away from the legal proceedings, that would have been so painful and traumatic for me. That I will never forget. You have been a good fiend, too. I am glad it's over, and I found a way to perpetuate Jennifer's memory, by helping other people carry on with something that was so dear and unique to her and to me, that she was never able to finish. Oh God, I am so thankful, a great load has been taken off me, and thanks to you Erica, for a happy closure."

With the settlement behind them, Jim and Erica worked very hard for the next five days.

Erica divided her time between the workstation in her bedroom and the main office downstairs.

Jim was very busy going over the daily report he was receiving from the Brussels office. He needed all data available to make his final report before his departure for the U.S. Jim, although based in London, oversaw the Brussels operations, too. With the expected growth, he planned to make a proposal to the board when back in the States, to appoint a separate director for the Brussels operations, and possibly open a new office in Amsterdam.

Jim and Erica saw each other only at suppertime. They went out to dinner twice, but both liked the comfort and informality of dining in. Either Jim cooked, or had food sent in. For the little time they had after supper and before going to bed, talked and enjoyed each other's views and interests. They found that both liked all kinds of music but preferred classical.

They promised themselves that Friday, the eve before Erica's departure, work done or not done, to spend some time carefree, and away from work pressure.

Jim and Erica had their Friday evening out, and returned to the apartment around 7 o'clock. Happiness and smiles were painted all over their faces. There was no doubt, they had a good time and enjoyed each other's company. Jim helped Erica take off her black raincoat and hung it in the closet.

She wore a short red and black plaid skirt, a red turtleneck cashmere sweater, black knitted tights, and ankle length black boots with short heels. She looked stunning. Her beauty was timeless and devoid of style, structure, or fashion trends. Whether in blue jeans or a custom-made business suits, her appearance remained unadulterated, ethereal, wondrous, elegant, and classy.

They sat on the sofa and put their feet up on the coffee table.

"That's set. Tonight is my last night in London. I had the greatest time of my life. I became the kid I never was. We had our formal dinners out and played host to each other, but tonight it was really fun. We went out for pizza like all school buddies."

"I had a fabulous time, too. I love your new outfit. It makes you so young and carefree. When did you have time to go shopping? You were either in the office or the apartment working like crazy all week long."

Erica laughed, shook her head several times in dismay, and in a very patronizing voice said,

"Jim, I am so sorry. It really shows. You haven't been around a woman for a long.....long time. Women always have time to go shopping, unless in jail or dead! And especially find time to go shopping for something they don't need. Shopping can provide all kinds of experiences; therapeutic, metaphysical, extraterrestrial, liberating, psychedelic, and even sexual! Some women claim that they have found G-spots in department stores and boutiques! The more exclusive and expensive they are the higher the intensity! And the sign 'Sales' for others is an 'upper;' for the weak at heart a path to absolution. By the way Jim, I like this outfit, too. I am going to wear it on the plane tomorrow."

"Your off the cuff remarks can blow anybody's mind away. They're an amalgam of parody, allegory, exaggeration, and humor. And I don't mean to flatter you or tell you something you're not aware of, Erica. I haven't met any man or woman with such a quick mind. I love it. By the way, what time are you flying out?"

"2:30 in the afternoon. I left several memos in your office. If you have any questions call me. I also plan to call you periodically for updates."

"I am thirsty. I am going to get a glass of water. Would you like me to bring one for you?"

"Please do. I am getting thirsty, too."

Jim went to the kitchen and came back, holding two glasses

of water. He offered one glass to Erica, and while standing started drinking.

"Jim, why are you standing? Sit down," Erica said, while looking at her watch. "It's only 7:30. The day is still young. Let's talk."

Jim sat down on the sofa, next to Erica and asked,

"Since we met in the States and here, I expressed my innermost deep feelings and thoughts. Do you think I was over sentimental?"

"Not at all. You were honest and wanted me to be aware how you felt about Jennifer and the uniqueness of your relationship. For me it was a revelation that two people could reach such a state of closeness and communion. I personally never have and to be honest with you, I don't even know if it's good for me."

"Let me ask you something that comes to my mind all the time. You are beautiful and smart. I am sure there are plenty of professional men who would die to get to know you better. Don't you think it's possible to meet a man, fall in love, and get married? Don't you miss the warmth of being close to another person, and I don't mean this strictly in the physical or sexual context?"

"You are not the first man or woman to ask me these questions. I think by now, we know each other well. For Heaven's sake, we have been living in the same house for one week. I will open up, and I hope you will understand.

Since I was ten years old, the only thing I knew, the only thing that drove me, the only thing that mattered, and the only thing that elated me, was how to excel and succeed. Remember that there is a very profound difference between being lonely and insular. The lonely is sad and wishes he or she had company and to be with other people. The insular is alone by choice. You and I are insular by choice. We could date and meet people if we wanted, but we don't. We have deliberately created a space around us that honors and respects our privacy, controls what comes to us, what stays with us, and what becomes part of us. By the way, Jim, don't even think that I dislike men or I am a hardcore feminist. One of my assets as a person is my femininity. I don't flaunt it, but I treasure it.

"I admire the depth, the sequence, and the expression of your logic, but you sound a little bit self-centered."

"You are right. My logic is for me, and not intended for anybody else. For the next three years, my only priority is to become the top corporate lawyer in the city. Jim, in you I have found a good friend. Us being together for a week has helped me discover qualities in a man that I respect and admire."

"And what are these qualities?"

"Your capacity to love and the depth of your love. The way you expressed your feelings for Jennifer unleashed a full range of dynamics in the scale of love. It was like a song with lyrics from a poem, where the composer and the poet merged their hearts and minds, and if notes were separated from words, both became meaningless."

"Wow! You know something? For somebody who hasn't been in love like you, you articulated the feelings of someone who has very well."

"You don't needs brains to sense the quality, depth, and above all the strength and redeeming power of love. Although I haven't been in love, my mind and heart with their analytical, visionary, and perceptive sensors created and conceptualized the perfect image that would depict the love that possessed you and Jennifer.

It' would be like an old dependent lighthouse that stood the test of time. It would guide you to a safe harbor through the worst storm, if the captain and the pilot-you and Jennifer-had the courage, faith, determination, and trust each other to follow trough. Jim, I think, I am going to start packing."

"It would be redundant to make any reference concerning your looks. What you have up in your head Erica, is something more beautiful and extraordinary-your mind! Your heart couldn't fall behind. Whoever taps them both would be the luckiest man of all time. I really enjoyed our talk tonight. For tomorrow, I have already called a cab. It will be here around 12 o'clock."

The next day, Saturday at 11:55 in the morning, Jim and Erica left the apartment and took the elevator to the lobby. The cab arrived as Jim was carrying the luggage outside. The driver took the suitcase and the carry-on bag and put them in the trunk, while Jim and Erica took the back seat.

On the way to the airport Erica and Jim were quiet for sometime, then Erica suddenly turned her head, looked at Jim and said,

"You know I am busy, and so are you, but I wouldn't mind if I had stayed for another week. I wished we had more talks like last night."

"You took the words out of my mouth. We were so busy. I feel so bad. I didn't even take you out to see a play."

"I didn't care too much about entertainment. Communicating, exchanging ideas, and learning about other people's lives, makes us more alert and changes our perceptions about our own lives."

At the airport, after Jim helped Erica check in, it was time to say goodbye.

Erica hugged Jim and said,

"Thanks for everything. I hope I can reciprocate soon, when you come back home. Goodbye."

"It was my pleasure. You did so much for me. Have a nice trip. Thanks again, goodbye, and keep in touch."

"I will. See you soon, bye-bye."

CHAPTER THREE

LOVE REDUX

Erica, after saying goodbye to Jim, took the escalator to the second level. She passed through security, then walked to the waiting area and took a seat. Thirty minutes later, boarding for first class passengers was announced.

Erica approached the gate, showed her boarding pass and passport, and proceeded to board the plane. She walked to the first class and one of the flight attendants placed her carry-on bag in the overhead bin, and hung her coat. As Erica took her window seat, another flight attendant carrying newspapers asked her,

"Ms. Hofmeister, would you like a copy of London Times?"

"Yes I would, thank you."

Erica took the paper and read it for awhile. Later, her face was buried behind the paper- apparently she fell asleep. Suddenly, she awoke by the captain's voice heard on the PA system.

"Ladies and gentlemen, this is your captain speaking. We have reached thirty five thousand feet altitude. The sailing is going to be nice and smooth all the way home. Enjoy your flight."

Erica put the paper down, reclined her seat all the way, and kept her eyes closed.

This was a nice trip that gave her a total new perspective. This was the first time in her entire adult life that she kept exclusive company with a man for a whole week, day and night. They talked, ate, walked, worked, and slept under the same roof. Did she like it? Of course she did, but why? It was hard to tell. There was a certain feeling of comfort that was totally strange to Erica and difficult for her to define.

Jim was not your ordinary everyday man. He was good looking, educated, worldly and successful. Could she fall in love with a person like Jim? Would she marry a man like Jim? The answer to both questions was maybe. Now the most fundamental and important question for an extraordinary and complex woman like Erica was at what cost? What would she lose? What would she gain besides intimacy? Her singular life made her what she was. Did she have to change?

Barriers are counterproductive in any relationship, but what about boundaries that would allow her to be with and give to others, and also with herself alone whenever she chose, and if she needed to. Even in a working and balanced relationship, time alone would be productive and of tremendous value for an individual pursuing personal growth. By asserting her individuality, Erica could go back and give more in a relationship without feeling insecure, depleted or intellectually cheated. And the most important of all, she would be always in control of herself.

The past eight days were very unusual for Jim. He hadn't been in the constant company of a woman since Jennifer died.

Jennifer was a beautiful woman in her own right. Her unpretentious expression of innocence, vulnerability, kindness, grace, and her sweet smile made her loving, trustworthy and reliable. Her intelligence was never outwardly projected, but became obvious by the wisdom and depth of her thinking, and articulation of her ideas. Jennifer's intelligence was guided more by her heart and less by her mind.

Erica was the opposite. Her intelligence flowed out of her naturally and totally unrestrained, guided more by her mind and less by the heart, and her beauty was miraculously intertwined with her intellect.

To find another woman like Jennifer would be impossible, like winning a multi-state power ball twice in a row.

The question was could someone fall in love with a woman like Erica? The answer wasn't easy. The complexity of Erica's personality could be intimidating at first. By not being pretentious, she allowed you to communicate with her, but only to the level she chose. A more puzzling question was how Erica would respond to love not only physically but emotionally as well. How would she integrate her mind and intellect with her feelings of the heart, and at which one's expense? Her drive to always succeed and win big could blank her sensitivity and intuition.

Erica left three days ago and Jim was back to his routine.

There were files, a printing calculator, and papers scattered all over the dining room table. The CD stereo was on playing the intermezzo from Mascani's 'Cavaleria Rusticana.' The phone rang; Jim got up, turned the music off, and answered.

"Hello, Jim speaking."

"Hi Jim, how are you? This is Erica calling."

"I am fine. How was your flight? Are you all settled in?"

"My flight was fine. Today was my first full day in the office. What time is it in London? I hope is not too late."

"It's 11 o'clock. I never go to bed before midnight. This time is fine, if you want to call here."

"This helps a great deal. Here is 5 o'clock, and all my staff is gone. I usually stay until 6-6:30. Jim, I had a wonderful time in London. You were a fantastic host. I hope I can return the favor when you come back home. What I enjoyed the most was your company, and the opportunity to get to know you better. This was a total new experience for me and I liked it. I hope, I didn't mess up your schedule."

"You must be joking. Your presence broke the monotony

of the last three years. I found our conversations concerning life and relationships, very stimulating and reflective.

I would like to thank you again for your efforts and the successful outcome of the case. I hope my original reaction and my decision how to disperse the funds were not perceived as lack of gratitude."

"Not at all. You made a noble decision that will have a tremendous impact on the community and will help others."

"Erica thanks again. I enjoyed talking to you not as my attorney but as a friend."

"I feel the same. I will get back to you in a week or two. Goodnight"

"Have a nice evening, Erica. Bye-bye."

After the phone call was over, Erica took certain documents from her desk and put them in her briefcase. It was time to go.

She took the elevator to the third floor, turned left, and walked through the double garage door marked 'Reserved Parking.' The fourth car to the right was Erica's, a silver Porsche 911 Turbo. The car's dual, highly-polished, gold color-plated exhaust pipes, reminiscent of ceremonial trumpets of Elizabethan Court, heralded the raw and beastly power that had succumbed and surrendered to beauty, grace and finesse. There was a nameplate nailed on the wall: 'Reserved for Ms. Hofmeister.'

Erica unlocked the car, put her briefcase behind the driver's seat, got in, closed the door, put her safety belt on, turned her CD player on and drove away. The music she listened to was the choral intermezzo, the Humming Song, from Puccini's opera 'Madame Butterfly.' The original recording was over forty-five years old, but because of the timeless beauty of the artists' voices it was still popular.

This opera and especially the Humming Song, had a special place in Erica's heart. This was the first opera she ever attended, accompanied by her parents at the age of eight, six months before her father died. On their way home her father asked her what did she like the most from the opera.

"The Humming Song. Butterflies are silent when they fly. You admire them only when you glance at their striking colors. If they weren't, the Humming Song would make them not only being seen in beautiful colors, but also heard in glorious music."

Erica's parents looked at each other smiling and shook their heads in disbelief.

The Humming Song's melody of sadness and hope reflected Erica's mood tonight. As she was driving home and listening to the music, she felt somehow unsettled. *There is something wrong with me*, Erica thought. *Why I am full with happy anticipation when I plan to call Jim, and pensive and reflective after the call is over, wishing it had lasted longer? And when alone in my apartment, why I feel strange, preoccupied, and distracted, when reminiscing of my staying with Jim in London?*

In the past, being alone in my apartment was a joy. I am thirty-three year old mature woman, a successful attorney, and always in complete control, but not now. I have to admit it, whether I like it or not, that after having lived with Jim for a week I became aware of parts of my psyche that I didn't even know were in me. It is love? I don't know, I have never been in love or with a man, period. The only thing I know for sure is that I miss Jim, I like Jim, and I like to be around him. The way he expressed his deep love for Jennifer was a revelation to me. I never read any love stories, they are too tacky for me, but Jim's description of love, as an effusion of the heart and mind of two who become one, was enlightening. What are Jim's expectations from a woman? It's hard to tell. I wish we had talked more.

After Jim hung up, he turned the stereo back on and continued working for awhile but his concentration was gone. He got up, turned the music off, then he sat down on the sofa and started thinking. *This place is so different since Erica left. Her presence was so comforting. I miss her. Am I in love with Erica? It's hard to tell. Jennifer has been gone for almost three years. My desire to have a child remains strong. With Erica here, other directions and possibilities in my life surfaced. Did I become curious first of Erica's personality, character and logic, and then attracted to her after getting to know her better? Maybe. The fundamental premise remains though, what can a man offer to a cerebral woman like Erica that would compel her to give up some of her independence?*

Jim got up, paced a few times, and stared at the phone for a few seconds. He moved his right hand to about four inches from the phone, then quickly pulled it back. Later, long past midnight, with a great deal of hesitation, Jim picked the handset with one hand and dialed two numbers with the other. Then, he slammed the handset on the phone, as if a force compelled him to stop the call.

Jim was tense, anxious, and started perspiring. He waited for a while to make sure that he had regained his composure, then he went back to the phone and very slowly and methodically dialed and made a fourteen number trans-Atlantic phone call.

Erica had just gotten out the shower, and put her robe on. As she started drying her hair, the phone rang in the bedroom. She quickly left the bathroom and went to the bedroom to answer to phone.

"Hi, Erica speaking."

"Hi Erica, this is Jim. I hope I am not disturbing you. We spoke earlier, but I couldn't go to sleep until we talked again."

"Jim, I am glad you called. I wish we had talked more when I called you from my office. What time is it in London?"

"2:30 in the morning, but doesn't bother me. There is something in my mind that came into focus after your last call. I know we are two very different people, but I enjoyed your company and I missed you. When you were here all things somehow fell in place, but after you were gone I never felt the same. I am not a kid, and neither are you. I have paid my dues, have a successful career, well-defined directions in my life, and the maturity that goes along with it. When we first met, objectively speaking, I thought you were not only beautiful, but fascinating, intellectually stimulating, and a determined woman. When you stayed with me other qualities came into view, like your femininity; reserved but classy. Erica, I am fond of you and when I get back in the States I would like to see you and get to know you not only as my attorney, but as my close friend, too. If you have any reservations or feel otherwise please let me know now. Erica, are you still on? Did we lose connection? Erica, Erica can you hear me?"

Erica was all shook up. She put her left hand across her eyes, and stayed silent for a few seconds.

"We didn't lose connection. As a matter of fact, I've never felt so connected in my entire life. Jim, what you said is true for me, too. My life has not been the same since my return. I almost called you back from the office, but I was embarrassed and out of control. I am very happy thinking that in you, I have found a close friend. The prospect of being close to you and being able to continue our friendship makes me excited and happy. I am glad you called. A heavy load is off my chest. Jim, go to bed. It's getting late. Goodnight."

"I am glad we share the same feelings. Goodnight."

After the call, Erica laid down in bed with her hair still wet, and started thinking.

Oh my God, I can't believe it. Am I dreaming? Is this really happening? We both know but neither Jim nor I came up in front to say the magic words I love you. Does it make any difference? Absolutely, not. The word 'love' is so often used, just to justify and excuse a transient state of mind, heart or lust, that can tarnish its brilliance and make it shallow. I am an attorney, and a master at using, twisting, and manipulating words in order to win.

Erica could sense that she was happy but scared, too.

Always being in control of herself, she questioned whether she had the sensitivity to provide emotional support for Jim. She never loved a man and had never been with a man before; for no man she ever met had moved either her mind or her heart. For Erica this was the utmost of self-control. It never bothered her and she was proud of it. Erica, as a woman, knew well that she was endowed with female intuitive power, but she never had a chance to use it. As a woman's woman, she knew that she could do it if the right man came along.

Treasures buried are not treasures lost. Once unearthed, shine brilliantly in the light and can even blind the eye!

After his call to Erica, Jim was at peace with himself. For

the first time since Jennifer's death he realized that his life had taken a step forward. He was amazed that he was attracted to a woman so different from Jennifer. He wasn't sure how ready Erica was to share, or how communication would mature to communion. She needed to accept the fact that sharing is not attainable unless you give something up. Would her priorities change, or would her 'go for the kill' career as a lawyer prevail?

Two weeks later and after Jim finished preparing supper the phone rang. The stereo was paying the Back Street Boys song 'Show Me the Meaning of Being Lonely.' Jim lowered the volume and answered the phone.

"Hi, this is Jim."

"Hi Jim, this Erica calling. I love that song; it's one of my favorites. Like you, I love classical music, but some pop music delivers a pleasant and soothing sound, and lyrics you can relate to."

"How is my friend, Erica?"

"Your friend Erica is very happy. I feel closer to you every day. Neither of us alone can plan the final outcome or predict the future, but at least we have a chance to provide comfort, friendship, and companionship to each other. Jim, I know at least for me this sounds crazy, because I have never said these things before. You think I am different and unique, so are you."

"There is nothing more to say, Erica. I miss you terribly."

"Now I have great news for you. I am sure you will be pleased.

The $5 million settlement has been deposited in an escrow account at the bank. The account cannot be accessed until you come back to U.S. Now the really great news; we had a partners meeting yesterday and everyone was moved by your kindness and generosity. According to our contract, the law firm was to collect thirty-three percent of the settlement. That would have come up to around to $1.6 million. The partners unanimously decided to defer the entire legal fee and donate the money to the foundation. The firm's name would be engraved in perpetuity under your name as one of the founders and original donors to the 'Jennifer Woodman Foundation.' Not all lawyers are greedy, Jim."

"That's very generous and unheard of. Knowing how your mind works, you were the primary mover and shaker behind this decision. Yesterday I received a fax from the U.S. office. They want me back within ten days. My replacement has already arrived, and the moving company started packing the big stuff, except for some personal items I will pack and carry in a small suitcase.

I feel so different now compared to my state of mind when I left the States for London, a little over three years ago. The despair has been replaced by hope, and the unknown started becoming a little more defined. And the reason is you."

"I am happy we will be together soon. Fax me your itinerary as soon as possible. I am planning to take the day off for your arrival and pick you up from the airport. Goodbye, and have a nice and a safe trip."

"I will see you soon. Bye-bye."

The Boeing 747 from London arrived in the U.S. on time. Jim unbuckled his seatbelt, got up, picked up his briefcase from the overhead bin and deplaned. He walked through the long corridor and followed the sign for 'Immigration and Customs.'

He took the escalator to the lower level, and after picking up a cart, walked to the first carousel. Shortly, his suitcase came. He placed his briefcase and suitcase on the cart, and proceeded to the U.S. Immigration counter. Jim showed his passport to the uniformed officer who stamped it and said,

"Sir, proceed to Customs."

The Customs agent asked Jim if he had anything to declare.

"No, I don't," Jim replied.

"Welcome home, Sir," the officer said, while letting Jim pass through.

"Thanks, Officer. It's nice to be home again."

Nice to be home again! What great words, spoken for centuries by tired sailors, infirm explorers, and wounded warriors after successes or failures, defeats or victories! What glorious sounds of anticipation resonate! Hope, comfort, warmth, serenity, rebirth, love.

Jim started moving his cart following the sign 'Waiting Lounge, Restaurants, Ground Transportation.' As soon as he entered the lounge, he spotted Erica immediately. She wore the same outfit she had on her last night in London. She had a red scarf around her head, folded and partially covering her forehead, tied in the back with the long ends falling over her black raincoat.

Jim pushed the cart faster toward Erica. They hugged and exchanged a firm handshake.

"Jim, welcome home. Since the last time we talked, if not busy, all I could think about was your return back to U.S. How was your trip?"

Jim put his right arm around Erica's waist, pushed the cart with his left, and both started walking towards the exit.

"My trip was fine. Thanks for coming. I missed you terribly. You look as beautiful and elegant as ever, more radiant, and you have my favorite outfit on. Your hair is longer. I like it."

"I've never felt close to a man before. I have met many men socially and through work, but no one ever came close to you. Your sensitivity, depth, consideration, and devotion made me think about life, its predicaments, and fleeting nature."

As they went through the exit door, Erica said to Jim.

"Wait by the curb. I am going to bring my car. I am not parked too far."

After Erica left, Jim parked his cart against the building, took his briefcase and suitcase off the cart and went back to the curb to wait for her.

Shortly Erica arrived driving her silver Porsche. She lowered the window and asked Jim to come around.

"The door is unlocked. Put your luggage in the back. There is plenty of room."

Jim walked around the back of the car to the passenger's

door. He opened the door, put the luggage in the back, got in, shut door, and fastened his seatbelt.

"Wow! This is a nice set of wheels you got. I didn't think you were the type. I envisioned you as the classic dark colored sedan lady."

Erica lowered her sunglasses almost to the tip of her nose, made direct eye contact with Jim, and with a whimsical smile said,

"You are wrong, and you are sexist, baby. Toys are not only for boys."

She put her sunglasses back on and drove away with noticeable acceleration.

While Jim was still laughing, turned his head and asked Erica,

"Do you really need a 416 horsepower engine to get around town?"

"Of course not. The knowledge of possessing and controlling power and the discipline to not to use it, is the real thrill.

Power becomes a servant not a master, a captive not a captor, a slave not a tyrant, a subject and neither a King nor a Queen. Taming power requires more vigilance, sophistication and diligence than the tempting, intoxicating, and reckless use of it."

"Here is Erica's mind in full action."

"It's not me. Jim it's you that stimulates my mind and puts it to work."

"Before we go too far, do you know how to get to Home Suites Hotel? The company has reserved a suite for me. If you don't know, I have directions."

"What directions Jim? Are you nuts? Don't you remember? I took today off to prepare dinner and hoped to spend the weekend together. We have so many things to talk about. My apartment is large, three bedrooms all with their own bathrooms, and very accommodating. You were such a nice host in London. Please don't deny me the opportunity to reciprocate and for us to spend some time together. Jim if we just remain friends, I will treasure the experience as a fundamental part of my growth as a human being."

"Your invitation is accepted. I am sure you will be a fine hostess."

Erica drove her car, carefully observing speed limit and all traffic signs. After entering the garage of her apartment, she parked on the second floor. Jim carried his suitcase and Erica helped by carrying his briefcase. Both walked to the second floor lobby and took the elevator to the seventh floor where Erica's apartment was located.

Erica unlocked the door, walked in and held it, then she let Jim in.

The apartment was spacious, with hardwood floors, oriental rugs, and nice paintings on the walls. There were fresh flowers on the hall credenza, and the dining room table, which was set for two.

Jim looked around impressed.

"This is a beautiful place you have Erica, so well coordinated. It shows your impeccable taste."

"You are right. The decorator did the leg work to find what I like." Then she looked at her watch and asked,

"It's 4 o'clock. What time would like to have supper?"

"6:30, if it's okay with you."

"That's fine with me. Let me take you to your bedroom now, Jim. You need to rest."

With Jim gone to take a nap, Erica got busy preparing dinner. The glass top dining table looked elegant. The flower centerpiece was arranged with white lilies, mixed with some greenery, and two bird of paradise flowers in the middle. In front of each embroidered lace placemat there was a small crystal ball, half filled with water, and a large gardenia floating inside. Erica carried to the dining room table a crystal ice bucket filled with ice and a water pitcher that matched the goblets and water glasses. Later, she brought an opened bottle of white wine and placed it on the wine coaster. Erica's appearance this evening was archetypical of a composite high-class hostess, combining elegance, confidence, flair, and reserve. Erica could put you at ease though, lest over-whelming admiration compromise one's composure. Erica wore an ankle length silk gown, of light green color with white flowers printed on. The flared, three quarter length sleeves matched the hem of the dress, which when walking, showed her open back, short-heeled white satin shoes. The medium cut square décolleté revealed the finely chiseld symmetrical definition of her collarbones that would have made any sculptor's lifetime upper torso dream come true. Her auburn hair, parted in the middle, was combed back and held with two clips, with a gardenia pinned on the left side.

It was past 6 o'clock.

Jim walked into the dinning room as Erica, using ice tongs, took ice cubes from the bucket, put them in the water glasses and poured water over from the pitcher.

"Oh my, I am blinded by beauty coming from all directions. And the air is filled with something so refined and ethereal."

Erica picked up one of the crystal bowls and put it under Jim's nose.

"It's a gardenia, so delicate, like you Erica."

Erica put the crystal bowl back on the table.

"Thanks. Gardenia was my mother's favorite flower. My father, not only for her birthday and their anniversary but whenever possible, would surprise her with a gardenia hidden under her pillow. Jim, you can pour the wine, I will serve dinner."

Jim poured the wine. Erica made several trips to the kitchen carrying the salad bowls, vegetable bowl, breadbasket with rolls, and the dinner plates.

" You made so many trips. I should have helped."

"That's fine. You can help me cleaned up after dinner. Let's sit down."

Jim helped Erica sit first, then he sat down. She raised her wineglass to a toast.

"Jim, welcome back to U.S. and to my home. I am so happy we met."

"So am I, You helped me when I was down, and you have given me hope."

Both sipped wine, passed the bread rolls, vegetable bowl and started eating.

"The jumbo shrimp is excellent. So is the rice. I have never tasted shrimp like this before."

"I soaked them in beer with the shell on for one hour. Before I broiled them, I removed the shell and used it to make broth for the rice. I am just a serviceable cook, but when I cook I like to be creative. Cooking is like making music. It is not only the sound that counts, but also how the sound is made. Two different artists can play or sing the same music, but they don't sound alike. By the use of different dynamics and nuances in performing the same musical score, artists can distinguish themselves by giving an individual and idiomatic texture in their performance that is characteristically theirs. The same is true in cooking. Two cooks can use the same ingredients or even the same recipe, but the food doesn't taste the same, and the texture can be different."

"You are fascinating. Your analogy depicts not only your critical and analytical mind, but your wit as well. Let me help you clean up."

Jim picked up dishes and silverware, and followed Erica to the kitchen. After they finished, Erica put her arm around Jim's waist.

"Jim, let's go to the living room."

Erica sat on the sofa and Jim on a lounging chair right across from her.

"The meal was excellent. Forget about dessert, not even later. Thanks again for a wonderful dinner. Let me ask you honestly, were you surprised with my last call from London?"

"Not at all, Jim. You beat me by one day. I had planned to call you the next day. I could sense that we were comfortable with each other. There is no question, we are different, but by being together for a week we found out, that although private and self-contained, we were able to freely communicate."

"Don't you think a man could feel overpowered or intimidated by you?" Jim asked.

"Did I overpower you? I don't think so," Erica answered.

"What I am finding out in general is, that my communication with others, men or women, drift to a different level that they aren't comfortable with."

"Have there been times or moments in your life that you've thought of getting married and having a family?"

"Of course. Every woman has at some point in her life. The question is at what price. When you give up part of yourself and get very little or nothing in return, you feel depleted and lose your balance as an individual."

"If you think of marriage, even as a remote possibility, you have to date and meet men beyond the social and professional scene."

"What about you? You haven't dated since you wife died. The way I look at it today, dating is a parody. Most men expect women to sleep with them, at least after the second date. If they don't, they are 'frigid' or 'mixed up' sexually. Take a look at the entertainment culture like TV; mature, educated, and beautiful people have a drink or attend a party, and in the next scene you see them in bed, with nothing ever happened in between.

Certain men and women nowadays have reached an evolutionary state of de-cerebration in which all neural pathways responsible for transmitting impulses from the brain have been disrupted with the exception of those located below the waist.

Women are not dummies. They know that possess a powerful weapon; sex, and most of them, depending on the circumstances, use it to attain specific objectives, and pleasure is not always one of them. Single women date and exchange sex for the hope and the prospect of getting married. If they don't, could lose their man and have to start all over again. By admitting being in love, whatever that means to them, sex becomes idealistic and romantic. Prostitutes exchange sex for money, and married women use or withhold sex in and out of marriage for revenge, punishment, to escape boredom, or to reaffirm their attractiveness.

"Don't you think you are generalizing, and your are judgmental?"

"I said certain and most, not all. Besides, this is my opinion, and I call it as I see it. Even the best referees can make mistakes. I am not a prude or against sex. Everybody makes his or her own decisions. A. C. Green, the former L. A. Lakers star, who married at the age of thirty-nine said in an interview, 'Sex was definitely worth the wait. The quest was something personal.' I am not a bitter or shriveled-up old maid. I am young and beautiful, so they tell me. What is important to me is that I am always in control of myself not only for the sake of power, but for the sake of grace and dignity."

"Again your opinions reaffirm your strong personality, and the concept of the individual, like yourself, being in control. Let's come close to home now. We know and have admitted that we are attracted to each other. What is your vision for us?"

"I have been doing all the talking. Why don't you tell me your vision?" Erica asked.

"With your demeanor, intelligence, and beauty, you can do anything you want, be with, and choose the best man around. From what I can see, your main concern has been all along, that beauty and the feminine part of you would prevail in the eyes of a man at the expense of you as person with a strong mind. I think the way I look at you and our ability to communicate with depth should take this fear away from you."

"Oh Jim, that's bull's eye. My looks are not my doing, but they can do me in. Us communicating freely made me see you, and especially myself and my needs as a person from a totally different angle."

"Even fools know that beautiful people are a plenty, sharp minds are not. The way your mind works feeds mine, and I hope I do the same for you. The way we complement each other gives me a clear and positive vision for our future," Jim said.

"I agree with you. Physical beauties were born to die, sharp and creative minds were born to live. If you hold a skull in one hand that belonged to a beautiful face and skull in the other, that belonged to a beautiful mind both look alike. What makes the difference is what was left behind. The beautiful face left nothing. The beautiful mind left everything. Any museum, library, concert hall, theater stage or opera house, from the very big and famous to the very small, attest that sharp and creative minds live in perpetuity, to inspire and stimulate the birth of new excellence."

Jim stood up, approached Erica, took her right hand, and as she got off the sofa, gave her a quick hug.

"Thank you for a wonderful and stimulating evening. I am getting tired, I am ready to go to bed, goodnight, and thanks again."

"Goodnight Jim. The pleasure was mine."

Jim stayed at the Home Suites Hotel for six weeks while he went apartment hunting. He found a two bedroom furnished apartment that met his present needs well. He wasn't ready to commit to purchasing anything residential at time of his life.

He was very busy with his new job as vice president of overseas operations and development, and with the foundation he established in his wife's memory. To avoid any perception of impropriety or conflict of interest, Jim declined the offer to become president of the foundation.

Steve Larson, his company president, was elected president of the foundation and Jim accepted the position of member of the board. Steve made a personal one hundred thousand dollar contribution to the foundation after his appointment as president. Jim's company allocated space and human resources to run the finances, and the University Fertility Center provided an office-staffed with a social worker and a psychologist for screening prospective infertile married couples applying for an in vitro fertilization grant.

Everybody was pitching in, including Erica and her law firm, with a great deal of enthusiasm, to ensure that all proceeds and income from the foundation would be used to help infertile couples who couldn't afford infertility treatment. With the cost per procedure running close to twenty thousand dollars, the foundation hoped to have enough revenues after a year to finance a minimum of twenty proccedures.

Erica's working schedule was full and hectic. She traveled throughout the U.S. constantly to meet with new and old corporate clients of her law firm and to address volumes of problems. Her capacity for critical analysis, decision logic, and recommended action intrigued and bewildered quite a few seasoned corporate executives. Her composite mind and adherence to details that escaped others would articulate opportunities and momentum that reached beyond corporate legal banality, and stimulated lovely, productive, and intelligent conversations.

Young single, good looking executives drooled over Erica, but her icy deep green eyes held them at bay in desperation. Her looks, business demeanor, and acumen earned her the epithet 'Executive Madam.' Her total commitment and preoccupation with her work was obvious to everyone who came in contact with her.

Jim and Erica met periodically, but because of Erica's extensive traveling their contacts were carried primarily over the phone. They accepted the fact that by destiny and circumstance were bound for life. Their courtship slowly developed to a full blown love of mind and heart, more spiritual than physical at this time; rather anachronistic by contemporary ethic and standards, but very rewarding and nurturing for them.

Jim was back in U.S. for three months. Friday evening, after leaving the office, he went to the car dealership to pick up the new car that he had ordered one week before he left London. It had finally arrived. It was a 4.0 S-Type light blue metallic Jaguar. Erica was in town and Jim planned to surprise her when he would pick her up for their Saturday evening dinner out.

It was drizzling, cloudy, chilly; a typical late fall, Midwest evening. Jim drove and stopped the car right outside the main entrance of Erica's apartment. She came out of the door, waved and said,

"Jim, don't get out, just unlock the door, I am coming right in."

She ran out of the apartment, stopped and checked the back of the car for a second, then got inside and closed the door.

"Jim, you are a stinker," Erica said laughing.

"You never told me you ordered a new car. I like the color, light blue. The color of clear and open skies."

"I ordered the car one week before I left London. I wanted to surprise you. What were you doing looking at the back of the car in this kind of weather?"

"I wanted to see if you got the three or four liter engine. I am glad you got the four. You have 41 extra horses, from two hundred-forty to two hundred eight-one."

"Erica you drive me nuts. You are a high power corporate attorney. Don't you have enough on your mind? Why bother with this kind of junk?"

"Oh, Erica would never allow herself to be made fun of twice."

"What do you mean?"

"Well, I was with the firm for six months. When I went to the boardroom for a meeting, the guys had opened car brochures and were talking about new cars. One smart big mouth offered to help me with technical information, if I was in the market for a new car! I thanked him, left the room, and went back right before the meeting started. Within two months I knew all specifications, like power train, engine size, dimensions, weight, tires, etc., of every domestic or foreign car marketed in U.S.A. A great part of our brains remains unused during our lifetime. Adding a little more information Jim, couldn't hurt."

"Erica, you are one of a kind," Jim said, shaking his head.

Jim stopped the car under the covered entrance of Coq d' Or, a nice French restaurant. He opened the door and got out, as the parking attendant went to the other side and opened the passenger's door to help Erica out. Erica walked to Jim and embraced his arm as the attendant handed him the parking ticket.

Jim and Erica walked to the entrance. The attendant opened and held the door, until both entered the restaurant lobby.

Jim checked his and Erica's coats with the female attendant at the cloakroom, saved the claim tickets, and confirmed the dinner reservations with the hostess. She took them to the table and handed the menus.

"Miss., Mr. Woodman enjoy your dinner."

"Thanks Miss."

Jim helped Erica sit before he took the seat across from her. His eyes were transfixed on Erica. He thought she was the all-time beauty. She had a deep maroon colored dress on that contrasted her unblemished skin of face and neck to perfection and gave it an alabaster shine. With the lights dimmed, her green eyes reflected a deeper shade, and the unnoticeable make-up projected a real, pure, natural, and unaccentuated beauty.

"Jim, this is a beautiful place, elegant and classy."

Jim took Erica's hand and smiled.

"No, you are beautiful, elegant, and classy. You are so radiant, a shining star in this gloomy, dreary day. Looking at your deep green eyes I am reminded of serene green pastures, where hope, understanding, and infinite love will graze, grow, and mature, in order to sustain us."

"We have been seen each other for three months since you came back, but tonight, for the first time you defined our love as infinite. Jim, I know from your past, that your capacity for love is endless. You past love does not make me either insecure or jealous, but reassures me of a seamless transition and continuity."

The waiter brought the wine list and asked if they would like something from the bar.

"Not for me. Jim, go ahead; order a drink if you like. I am ready to order my meal."

"So am I."

Jim and Erica ordered, and shortly the waiter brought the salads and bread rolls.

"Erica have you talked to anyone about us?"

"No, you know me by now Jim. I treasure my privacy and never discuss my personal life with others."

The waiter brought and served the main course, took away the salad bowls, and both started eating.

"Neither have I. I am so content with my life, only sharing with you matters."

Later, the waiter showed them the dessert list, but both felt pleasantly full and declined. Jim paid the bill and he and Erica, holding hands, walked to the cloakroom to pick up their coats. Jim helped Erica with hers, and both walked out. Jim handed the parking ticket to the attendant, and shortly his car was pulled up to restaurant door.

Jim tipped the attendant, helped Erica get in the car and drove away.

Driving to Erica's apartment, both were in a state of total silence. Erica rested her head on Jim's left shoulder and kept her eyes closed.

Silence is the absence of sound, and sound is the absence of silence. Both cannot be synchronous, but define, proceed or follow each other.

Thunderous, high-energy sound could be followed by a state of contemplated silence, or a state of contemplated silence could be the precursor of a booming earthquake sound that either separates or fuses.

All relationships, as they go through various phases of maturity, have defining moments of silence and sound that either make them stronger, weaker, or take them apart.

After parking the car in the garage, Jim and Erica walked to her apartment. Their facial expressions radiated tranquility and contentment. Their eyes crossed and stared at each other as they took off their coats. Erica, after hanging them in the hall closet, put her arms around Jim's neck and kissed him tenderly.

"I am glad you came up to be with me. I know how busy you have been since you came back."

Jim kissed Erica back, put his arm around her as they walked to the living room and sat on the sofa, very close.

"I had a wonderful time tonight. Jim, I feel so close to you. I never believed that such happiness would to be part of my life."

Jim rested his head on Erica's shoulder and remained silent for a minute or two. It seemed like an eternity for a heart in longing and a mind in consenting. Jim lifted his head, took both Erica's hands in his, looked her directly in the eyes, bit his lower lip once, opened his mouth wide, and took a deep breath.

"Erica, I love you with all my heart. You are my only hope for happiness now and in the future. I will love you forever. I wasn't"...

Jim stopped and became emotional. Erica let her hands go, and put them on Jim's face, moving her head close to his.

"Jim I love you, your are the only love in my life. I have never loved before. You have, and you taught me what unconditional love is. I have started living it. Unconditional love changes you, liberates you, and purifies you."

Jim kissed Erica on the lips once and took a deep breath again.

"I wasn't...I wasn't planning to ask you tonight, but my love for you is so overpowering. Will you marry me, my love?"

Erica started crying and kissed Jim several times.

"Oh yes, I will marry you. Please, don't say another word. Let silence reign. Let me hold you, and you hold me. This is the sweetest and most peaceful moment of my life. I feel as light as a feather drifting in the balmy breeze of a summer dawn. I don't know how these words come to my head, and out of my mouth. And I don't remember the last time I had tears in my eyes."

After Jim left, Erica went back to the living room and sat on the sofa. Erica the Cool not only was in love, but accepted a marriage proposal without a second thought. Did she lose control? Did she act out of character? Was her resolve gone? Was her individuality in the process of being compromised?

Erica thought very carefully and logically, and the answer to these questions was a categorical, no. Her heart was happy and her mind wasn't threatened. Erica was convinced that if she was ever to get married, no one could fill Jim's shoes. He, as a professional himself, would understand the demands of her work, especially for the next two to three years, and he would be a very supportive partner.

It's in the nature of inquisitive minds to have doubts but will never allow them to block the decision-making process, which is exclusively their domain.

Erica was happy, either by coincidence or fate, that for the next two weeks she hadn't scheduled any traveling. That would give Jim and her more time to be together, plan for the future, and most importantly celebrate their love.

Tomorrow, Sunday, Jim had to be in the office for at least six hours to do some catching up, but he promised Erica that he would visit her in the evening and spend some quality time together.

It was Sunday around 6 o'clock.

Erica just took out of the oven a chocolate cake she baked for this evening. She turned the coffee maker on, and carried china, silverware and napkins to the living room and put them on the coffee table. She wasn't nervous at all, but she was exited for sure. Her fiancé was coming for a visit. That was an event that would be part of her life until the very end.

Erica went to her bedroom to change. She took off her T-shirt and blue jeans, walked in her closet and looked around. She wanted to put on something cheerful and playful to make her femininity shine, and lighten up Jim's mood.

She chose a coral colored poplin shirt accented with a white collar and white French cuffs, and a designer's denim, mid-calf length skirt embroidered at random with small coral color flowers. She had matching open back shoes with cork wedged heels. She brushed her hair and started getting dressed. She put the shirt on first, leaving unfastened the first two buttons, and stepped into her shoes, after putting on a new pair of pantyhose. Then, she put the wraparound skirt, with the opening over the left leg, and tied the one-inch attached belt, in a bow right in front. She checked her face in the mirror, put her perfume and light make up on, and took out of the jewelry box a pair of pearl cufflinks and her gold Rolex watch and put them on.

    Erica was aware of and loved her femininity. From now on, her femininity would go beyond pleasing herself. It would be part of Jim's delight.

    The doorbell rang and Erica rushed to the door. She opened it, and there was Jim holding a bouquet of red roses and a bottle of Bollinger champagne.

    "Erica, let's celebrate more formally tonight. I wasn't prepared last night. You look so beautiful, and happy."

    Erica hugged and kissed Jim, took the flowers and the champagne and put them on the hall credenza.

    "Jim, what happened last night was purely magical. Your spontaneity was godsend, and the lack of formality made the event even more heartfelt. Don't get me wrong. I love champagne and flowers, but what we have is so original and unique; it defies social etiquette and conventionality. Jim I am putting the roses in a vase and the champagne in the refrigerator."

    "Can I help?" Jim asked.

    "No, thanks. I will take care of everything. Go to the living room, sit down and relax. Too bad, you had to work to day."

    Jim walked to the living room and sat on the sofa. Erica took the bottle and the flowers and carried them to the kitchen. She put the bottle in the refrigerator and the roses in a vase, carried them to the living room, and put them on the coffee table.

    "The roses are so beautiful and fresh like our love."

    Jim raised both hands, in a quote unquote gesture.

    "Erica, for an austere corporate lawyer you sound very

romantic. On the other hand, your intelligent mind moves quickly to so many different levels, you always come up with uncanny metaphors, allegories, analogies, and observations."

Erica fell on her knees, took Jim's right hand with both of her hands, looked him in the eyes, smiled, and in affected, refined, and accented English said,

"Erica, Maiden in waiting, she shall not be for long my Lord, for Queen she shall be crowned." Then she kissed Jim's hand.

Jim pulled Erica up, kissed her, and both laughed to tears.

"Where is that from Erica?" Jim asked.

"I don't know. I guess, I just made it up."

"You are an amazing woman, with an amazing mind and I love it all."

"Jim I baked a chocolate cake and brewed fresh coffee. We can have the brut some other time. From now on, we will have many occasions to celebrate."

"That's fine with me. I love chocolate cake."

After they finished having coffee and cake, Jim carried dishes and silverware to the kitchen, and helped Erica clean up. Both content and happy came back to the living room and sat on the sofa.

"Your cake was delicious. Very moist, and the right thickness of frosting."

"Thanks; it was nice sharing it with you. From now on, sharing everything with each other will make us better persons and expand our love.

Jim until yesterday, my career was the most important thing in my life. Since last night you are. I will love you forever and try to meet all your needs. I don't know if you recall, we had discussed this before. I deeply understand your longing for a child, but I would like to wait for at least two more years before we start a family. My corporate practice, that I love, is so demanding I can't do both. Nowadays, many professional women start a family in their middle or even late thirties."

"I remember well, and I admire you for your intellectual honesty."

"Since we won't try to have a family now, I will continue taking birth control pills."

Jim's face became flushed, appeared disturbed, and tried to restrain his anger.

"Wait a minute. What is this all about? You told me you had never been with a man, and after I proposed, you tell me you are on the pill. That's totally absurd. I don't know what to believe any more."

Erica remained assured, calm, and composed.

"What I told you was the truth. I will never lie to you. Please, hear me out. My grandmother, on my mother's side and my mother's older sister died from ovarian cancer. There is a genetic link. If you have two direct blood line relatives like myself who died from the disease your chances to die from the same disease is higher than average. The risk falls back to average if you take birth control pills. Since I had my first period at the age of fourteen my gynecologist prescribed birth control pills. This won't interfere with having children later. After two years I will stop the pill and nature will take its own course."

Jim covered his face with both hands.

"I am so sorry. I am so embarrassed and I feel like a fool."

Erica kissed Jim several times smiling.

"Don't be silly. Forget it. We have more important things to talk about. I would like to start our lives differently. We don't have to do stuff for the sake of being appropriate and socially right. To begin with, don't even think about it. I do not want an engagement ring."

"I was planning to take you to jewelry store tomorrow."

"I know you can afford it, and you want to give me one. I never wear any jewelry, unless there is some formal occasion. I have two large diamond rings, my mother's and my grandmother's, both sitting in my bank's safety deposit box. That's plenty."

"Okay, I will get you something original, just for you."

"That I like. I want every thing about us to be original. Now, let me tell you my plans for our wedding. If you have any different ideas, cut in at any time.

I believe in God, but I haven't attended any particular church on a regular basis, like you and Jennifer did. We will do that after we get married. For our wedding service, choose any church you are comfortable with. I would like our wedding ceremony to be as private and simple as possible. Aunt Mary, who raised me, would have been my only guest, but she is dead. I won't wear a formal bridal gown or train. I will find something elegant but simple. The only jewelry I am going to wear is my family locket from my mother's side of the family."

"Erica, not only do I like, but I love your plans. I will have only one guest myself, Stanley-he is a pharmacist, my closest friend from high school. We are like brothers. He was my best man the first time I got married and I will ask him to be our best man again. And if it's okay with you, I would like us to get married in the same church."

"That's fantastic. What a continuity of love, grace, and commitment. Our wedding wouldn't be a spectacle or a show, but the initiation of our communion."

"Now tell me more about your family's gold locket," Jim asked.

"Well, it has been in our family for some time. It has the shape of a rose. When you open it, you see pairs of names engraved, brides and grooms, and below that the date of their wedding. My parents, grandparents, and great-grandparents names are in and the date they got married. There is one space left for us."

"What a beautiful family tradition."

"Something else. I don't care for honeymoons. We will have plenty of time to travel. I will redecorate the master bedroom, and get all new furniture. It's going to be our bridal suite, our honeymoon suite. I am glad you decided to make this our home. For the time being it is exactly what we need, and I have an extra parking space you can use."

"Your plans couldn't be any better. Something private, something original. That's us, that's our wedding. I love you, Erica."

Two months had past since Jim and Erica got engaged, but time appeared to bear no relevance. It felt as it if they had been together all their lives. Both continued their demanding carriers with outstanding vigor and energy. What amazed them was that when together, that part of their lives not only faded away, but did not even exist.

Love and commitment to each other became a fortress and an armor that constantly protected them from common trivialities in the process of building their own unique kingdom. Skepticism and doubts, the welcome intruders of sophisticated and inquisitive minds visited, inquired, conversed, argued, but left happy, with all questions addressed and logically answered.

The perfectly balanced hearts and minds in Jim and Erica's singular state were able to adjust their individual boundaries, to allow constant crossing over with neither guilt, compromise, nor depravation. The individual balance of heart and mind became a collective balance with a seamless transition.

Today, Jim and Erica got married. The service was exactly as they had planned and wished for. Private, unobtrusive, spiritual, contemplative and unique, reflecting their own combined state of love, happiness and individuality. After the service and dinner, both returned to Erica's apartment that would become Jim's home, too, from now on.

Once the door opened, Erica and Jim walked in. The sight was of a composite portrait of life and art, aesthetics and form, accomplishments and rewards.

Erica wore a designer's white long-sleeve organza dress, lower calf-length, with four inches ruffle at the hem and a two inches ruffle around the neck and wrists. The shoes she had on over fine white pantyhose, were white kid leather pumps, with two and one half-inch heels. She had white gloves on, and was holding a bouquet of white roses. Her hair combed up and held back, exposed her long neck and made her upper torso look more statuesque. Erica wore a gardenia crown placed one inch below the hairline in front, and crossing the upper part of her head in the back. She had around the neck a gold chain holding the family locket that hung in front. If, at this very moment, time had stood still in its infinite course, Erica would personify the epitome of a multidimensional beauty in her glorious victory of life. Jim looked dapper in his black suit, white French cuff shirt, and silver color silk tie.

Once in the hall of the apartment, Erica put the bouquet of white roses on the credenza and removed her gloves. The gold wedding ring, on her left ring finger shined. Jim approached her and kissed her neck. She turned around and they kissed on the lips, then kissed each other's wedding ring. Jim went to the living room, removed his jacket, tie, and unbuttoned the top button of his shirt. Erica followed him and sat on the sofa. Jim sat next to her and they kissed on the lips and cheeks several times.

On the coffee table there was a silver tray with two long-stem crystal champagne glasses that Erica had put out before they left for the wedding.

"Jim, I love you. You have changed my life forever. This was the most beautiful wedding I have ever attended. It was our wedding, so simple and intimate, so loving and elegant, so promising and pure"

"I love you. That's all I can say. No more shall be. You are my Queen now. I am going to bring champagne."

Jim got up, went to the kitchen, took the champagne out of the refrigerator and removed the cork. When Erica heard the pop, picked up one of the glasses and stood up. Jim returned to the living room holding the bottle, poured champagne in Erica's glass, and then in the other glass on the tray, and raised it to a toast.

"To my love, to my wife, to my Queen," he said, as both took their glass to their lips and sipped.

Then Erica raised her glass to a toast.

"To my love, to my husband to my King. Erica, Maiden in waiting no more my Lord, for Queen she is crowned."

"For goodness sake Erica, where is this from? Oh, I remember you answer from before: you don't know. You just made it up. You are amazing, even on your wedding night your mind doesn't rest. You can be profound, funny, and witty all at the same time. That's why I love you and respect you."

"My love for you connected my heart to my mind. Love empowers both, and loving and thinking are tuned to a perfect pitch."

"Before we left for church, I sneaked in the bedroom and left your wedding present. Would you like to see it?"

"Let's go. I can't wait."

Jim took Erica by the arm and went to the bedroom. In the middle of the bed there was a red velvet box tied with a white ribbon. Erica kicked her shoes off, sat on the bed, and picked up the box. Jim sat next to her. Erica untied the ribbon and opened the box. Her face lit up with a big smile. She took out of the box a large gold locket, shaped like a heart, with engraved rose petals on the surface, and attached to a gold chain.

"That's beautiful Jim. I love the roses."

"I know how much you love your family locket. Go ahead and open it."

Erica opened the locket that split to two half-hearts. Jim and Erica's names were engraved inside and below the weeding date was the inscription: The date our minds and hearts became one.

"That's so inspirational."

"Today, we started our own family locket, and the roses connect our family to yours. Erica, the family tradition has entered a new chapter of love; the love of minds and hearts."

"Thank you love," Erica said, and kissed Jim passionately.

She took her gardenia crown off, pulled out all the flowers and scattered them all over the bed. Erica and Jim continued to kiss with love, passion and desire, and blissfully surrendered to each other with the promise to live and love united with one sensitive heart, and think with one powerful mind.

Jim and Erica's personal and professional lives, after their marriage, were well balanced although both remained very busy.

Erica took Jim's last name and used her maiden name only as an attorney. Socially, at the present, they weren't active. With Erica's heavy travel schedule, both treasured each other's company and lively conversations that complemented and stimulated each other's intellectual curiosity.

In the four months they had been married kept the promise never talk about work or bring any work home. That would have been an emotional and intellectual intrusion and piracy that both objected to. Their minds and hearts felt adamant about it.

Accomplished professionals value and use own time wisely as a primary resource of inner building and growth. It they don't, become insecure, disorganized or unhappy.

CHAPTER FOUR

DECEPTION AND BETRAYAL

When Jim came back from a meeting it was past 12 o' clock. He found a note from Karen his assistant, taped on the phone:

"Mrs. Woodman called. She would like you to call her before you go to lunch. She is in her office. Karen."

Jim called Erica right away.

"Hi baby, what is up?"

"Jim, I am sorry to bother you. I am going to be late tonight. Would you please do me a favor? My gynecologist called and refilled my prescription for birth control pills. I am out. Would you please pick them up on your way home?"

"No problem. I will go now. I am going to be late, too. I have to make a presentation. Unfortunately, I forgot the dossier with all the information at home. I am sure that I left it on the dining room table. I have to go back, and on my way I will pick up your pills and put them in the medicine cabinet. Is there anything else we need? I know we need toothpaste."

"I am out of shampoo. That's all I need. I love you and see you later in the evening. Bye"

Jim left the office right away and drove to Stanley's drugstore. After parking the car, he went inside, picked up toothpaste and shampoo, and walked to the pharmacy counter.

"Hi, I'd like to pick up a refill prescription for my wife. The name is Erica Woodman."

The cashier brought the refill out and scanned all items.

"The total comes to $62.75. Credit, or cash?"

"Thanks, I will pay cash."

He took out his wallet, paid the bill, and the cashier handed him a plastic bag with the merchandise. After he left the drugstore, he drove home.

First he went to the bathroom and took out of the bag Erica's birth control pills and put them in the medicine cabinet. Then he put the toothpaste on the counter next to the sink, and the shampoo in the shower stall.

On his way out, Jim went to the dining room, picked up his blue dossier he needed for this evening's presentation, and drove back to the office

Jim and Erica celebrated their seven month wedding anniversary, with a quiet dinner at home. Erica's travelling was curtailed lately and wouldn't resume for an another four weeks. Both felt very close and happy, and as if they had been together for years, not seven months.

Erica and Jim were asleep. She lay on her left side. Jim was close to her back, with his right arm crossing over her torso. It was quiet, and the dark silence of the night was rhythmically interrupted by the sweetest music of all, the music of life; Jim and Erica's breathing sounds.

Suddenly the alarm clock rang. Erica woke up, turned it off, and very slowly moved Jim's arm away from her. She got up very quietly, and turned on the small lamp on the nightstand. Jim woke up, covered his eyes with his right arm and asked Erica,

"What time is it?"

"5:30," Erica answered

"What's going on? Why are you up so early?"

"I am sorry to wake you up. I forgot to tell you last night, I am going to the club this morning for my workout before going to the office."

Erica leaned over, kissed Jim, and pulled the blanket up to his shoulders.

"Jim, go back to sleep. I will be quiet. Since I don't have to go to the club after the office, I will be home early. I love you."

"I...love you, too," Jim said yawning.

Erica went to the bathroom to brush her teeth and hair, and wash her face. She turned the bathroom lights out and went back to the bedroom. She started doing some packing. She took out of her dresser drawer a pair of panties and pantyhose, a bra, a half-slip, a T-shirt, a pair of white anklets and put them on the chair next to the nightstand. She walked into her closet and took out a light beige two-piece running suit, a pair of white gym shoes, and a small overnight bag. She took off her nightgown and put the T-shirt and the running suit pants on. She went back to her closet and took out a business suit, a white blouse-both in drying cleaning bags, and a pair of dress shoes. After she packed the clean underwear and the dress shoes in the overnight bag, she put on the anklets, the gym shoes, and the jacket of the running suit.

Erica picked up her car keys from the nightstand, and put them in the right pocket of her running suit pants, where she had placed an envelope the night before. She turned the nightstand light out and left the bedroom carrying to her car the suit, the blouse, and the small bag.

She unlocked the driver's door, laid the suit and the blouse on the back seat, placed the small overnight bag behind the driver's seat, locked the car, and left. Shortly, Erica returned holding her briefcase. She unlocked the car with the remote control, opened the passenger's door, and placed the briefcase on the passenger's seat. She opened the briefcase, took out of the right pocket of the running suit pants the envelope she put in the night before, checked the contents –five one hundred dollar bills- and put them in the briefcase. Before she closed her briefcase, removed her wedding ring and put it inside. Erica got in the car, put the safety belt on, turned the ignition on, and slowly started driving towards the exit.

It was 6:20 in the morning and still dark.

Erica slowed down at the exit and made a right turn on 7th Avenue. She continued driving for about a mile, then she slowed down, and stopped at the intersection of 7th Avenue and Main Street, when the traffic light changed from yellow to red.

Erica put the left turn signal on, and when the light changed to green, she made a left turn on Main Street. She continued for about two miles, then stopped for a red light. When the light changed to green, she started moving forward.

Suddenly, a screeching braking, and almost instantaneously, a loud impact sound were heard. A SUV crossing failed to stop on time when the light changed to red, and hit Erica's car broadside on the right pillar and fender and dragged it about six feet sidewise and to the left. The windshield and the passenger's door window were shattered but not scattered, except for some small pieces inside and outside of the car.

Erica's head lay on the left pillar and her eyes were closed.

The traffic was blocked at the intersection, and within minutes, police cars, a fire truck, and an ambulance with paramedics arrived at the scene of the accident. A policeman and a firefighter holding an ax approached Erica's car. The policeman stooped over, looked through the window, and knocked hard with his right knuckles.

Erica, startled, opened her eyes, turned her head and stared at the policeman. He signaled her, with a rotating motion of his hand, to lower the window. She couldn't, but was able to open the door. Three paramedics came and placed a stretcher close to the car.

"Miss, are you alright?" the policeman asked.

"I feel fine, just a little dazed. What happened? I couldn't open the window. I have no power. My car is stalled."

"Madam, you were involved in an accident. It wasn't your fault. A SUV went through a red light and hit your car on the right side."

Erica turned her head to the right and saw the front of the SUV smashed into her car.

"Oh God, thanks. I am not hurt."

"Madam, the EMT crew is here. They will take you to the hospital."

One paramedic held Erica's head and neck still while another put a cervical collar around her neck. The seatbelt was unbuckled and with the help of a third paramedic, Erica was moved and placed flat on the stretcher. A rolled up pillow was placed on both sides of her neck to help immobilize the cervical spine. When Erica was laid on the stretcher, bloodstains were visible in her pants around her crotch and upper inner thighs. She was covered with a blanket, her vital signs were taken, and she appeared comfortable. The chief paramedic called the dispatcher of the ER at City Memorial Hospital and gave a brief report;

"We have a white female, in her thirties, involved in MVA. She is lucid, her vital signs are within normal limits, she is stable and not in acute distress. So far the only thing I can see is a little blood around her crotch area, over."

While Erica was being transferred to the ambulance, the ER dispatcher radioed back.

"I checked with the ER physician. Start an IV on your way to the hospital, and take the patient directly to the CAT Scan Suite for examination of the abdomen and pelvis, over."

The ambulance took off in a hurry for the hospital with the siren and flashing lights on.

A police photographer took pictures of the impact, and the inside of Erica's car. After he finished, a police investigator in street clothes searched the car. With the driver's door open, on the floor and in front of the passenger's seat, Erica's briefcase was seen. It was wide open. There were scattered documents, five one hundred dollars bills, and Erica's wedding ring.

The police investigator catalogued all items and made sure that photographs were taken before anything was touched. He placed everything in two large plastic bags including the briefcase, suit, blouse, and the small overnight bag, found in the back of the car.

After the CAT Scan was done, Erica was transported to the ER on a cart. Her IV was running to be kept open, and she was receiving oxygen through a small tube placed in her nostrils.

A doctor came in and asked the nurse,

"Sue, how is Mrs. Woodman?"

"She is fine, no changes Dr. Allen. Her vital signs have been within normal range all along."

Dr. Allen approached Erica smiling.

"Mrs. Woodman, I am the ER physician who examined you in the CAT Scan Suite and ordered your blood work. I am happy to tell you that all the tests were negative including the CAT Scan. The only positive finding on your physical examination was vaginal bleeding, but I did not do an internal examination. Under the circumstances, it should be done by a Gynecologist. I called a consultant. He is on his way"

"Thanks, Dr. Allen. I appreciate your concern."

"You are welcome. Mrs. Woodman."

Dr. Allen asked the nurse to remove the oxygen catheter, and as he was leaving the examining room, a voice was heard on the intercom.

"Sue, this is the front desk. Mr. Woodman is here. Can he come in?"

"Sure, send him in."

Jim came in. He looked worried and very concerned. He kissed Erica and held her hand, as the nurse walked out.

"Jim, stop worrying. Thank God, everything is fine. All the tests were negative. I have some vaginal bleeding. I am waiting for the specialist to give me an internal examination."

Sue, the ER nurse, came back to the examining room.

"Mr. Woodman, would you please step out. The specialist, Dr. Ferris is here."

Jim walked out of the examining room, and within seconds, Dr. Ferris came in and introduced himself.

"Mrs. Woodman, my name is Dr. Ferris, the gynecologist Dr. Allen called to examine you concerning your vaginal bleeding. Are taking any medications?"

"None, except for birth control pills."

"When was your last menstrual period? Are you regular?"

"A little over two months ago. Sometimes I am late, but this was the first time it has gone over two months."

"When was the last time you saw your gynecologist?"

"Less than a year ago, for my yearly physical examination. Everything was okay."

Dr. Ferris turned to the nurse;

"Sue, please put Mrs. Woodman on stirrups and get me the vaginal exam tray."

The nurse draped Erica's lower abdomen and legs, after putting the legs on stirrups. Dr Ferris adjusted the overhead headlight, put a pair of gloves on and did a vaginal examination. Then he inserted the speculum- an instrument to help him see better, picked up blood clots with a pair of forceps, and looked inside carefully. After he finished, removed the instrument, asked the nurse to put Erica's legs down, and bring Jim back into the examining room.

"Mrs. Woodman, I hope, I didn't hurt you," Dr. Ferris said, as he removed the gloves.

"Not at all."

As Jim walked in, Dr. Ferris shook hands with him.

"Mr. Woodman, I am Dr. Ferris. Your wife is fine. The bleeding was not from any injury to the female organs. Whether it was coincidental or induced by the stress of the accident is hard to tell." Then Dr. Ferris turned his head to Erica.

"Birth control pills are almost one hundred percent effective as a form of contraception. It's extremely rare- this is the first case I have seen in my twenty years of practice- but it can happen for a woman to conceive while on the pill. Have you had a pregnancy test done?"

Erica didn't respond, as she was thinking, then hurriedly answered.

"No, I haven't. I didn't have a reason to."

"Mrs. Woodman the size of you uterus, the bluish purple discoloration and the softness of your cervix are typical findings of pregnancy. You were about two months pregnant and you've had a miscarriage. This was the cause of the vaginal bleeding."

Jim appeared disturbed but tried to conceal his feelings with silence.

"Dr. Ferris, is it possible to be pregnant and have no other symptoms except for missing periods?"

"It is very possible."

"Mrs. Woodman, after a miscarriage, there maybe some residual tissues left that may cause bleeding or infection. It is important to ensure that your uterus is clean by scraping the inside. The procedure is simple, requires very little anesthetic, and you can go home after an hour or two. The procedure will have no affect at all if you would like to become pregnant in the future."

Dr. Ferris asked the nurse to go to the front desk and confirm Erica's procedure with the operating room and anesthesia. Later, the nurse came back to the room holding a brown sealed envelope.

"Mr. Woodman, this is the only valuable your wife had on, when she came to hospital. Would you please check it?"

Jim opened the envelope, found inside Erica's gold Rolex watch and asked the nurse,

"What about her wedding ring?"

"Don't worry Sir, I have it," answered a man as he walked into the room, holding two plastic bags. He went to Jim and Erica and introduced himself.

"My name is Lieutenant Malone, police accident investigator for the vehicular division. Mrs. Woodman, your ring was found outside your open briefcase, along with cash and other documents. Everything is inside these two bags including your clothes. I have made a list. Please check it, and after you sign it I will give you a copy."

Erica checked the list, signed it, and the lieutenant gave her a copy.

"Mrs. Woodman, you will receive a formal police report of the accident, but before I go, I would like to give you a quick update. The driver who hit you is the sixteen year old son of the owner of the largest car dealership in the city. The car is owned and insured by the car dealership. The driver was cited for speeding and failure to stop for a red light. Goodbye and I am glad you're doing all right."

"Thanks officer, so am I."

Erica was taken to the holding area, adjacent to the operating room, and examined by the anesthesiologist. He checked her IV to make sure it was open, and asked her questions concerning any known allergies to medications. Dr. Ferris, in his scrub suit, came in to say hello, and shortly she was wheeled to the OR.

After Erica was taken to surgery, Jim went to the waiting room. One hour later, Dr. Ferris came in.

"Mr. Woodman, your wife is fine. She will be ready to go home pretty soon. I suggest you take the elevator down to the first floor, and have a seat by the exit lobby. One of the recovery room nurses will escort Mrs. Woodman downstairs, when she is ready to be discharged."

"Thanks Dr. Ferris."

Jim took the two plastic bags with Erica's stuff, went to the first floor and waited for Erica.

Later, a double glass door opened and Erica came to the lobby sitting on a wheelchair, pushed by a nurse in a scrub suit. She looked relaxed and smiled. Jim got up and kissed her.

"I am glad it is over. I love you."

"So am I. I hope you are not disappointed."

"Erica, don't worry, it could have been worse."

"Mr. Woodman, why don't bring you car up in front by the curb. When I see you, I wheel your wife out," the nurse suggested.

"That's a good idea," Jim said and left.

He pulled up his blue Jaguar to the curb, got out, and opened the right front door. Both thanked the nurse, Jim helped Erica get in, then he got in the car and drove home.

When they got home it was about noon.

Erica went directly to the bedroom, removed her clothes and took a long hot shower. She wasn't physically tired, but felt numb all over. The steamy hot water was soothing, relaxing, and palliative.

She told Jim she would rest for a while, wasn't hungry for lunch, and would prefer something light for supper, like a cup of soup. Jim took the day off to be with Erica.

There was something unusual about Erica today, that Jim couldn't figure out. She was extremely pensive and not very talkative. Was it the accident or something else that she tried to put behind, forget and reconcile?

After supper, they went to the living room. Jim sat on the sofa, and Erica lay on her back, with her head resting on his lap. Jim played with her hair, while holding her left hand with his. They just finished listening to 'Summertime' from Gershwin's 'Porgy and Bess.'

"How sad, but so beautiful," Erica said.

"Sometimes, in this fleeting and unpredictable life, sad and beautiful go hand in hand. Today, it was a sad day. We lost our unborn child. But it was a beautiful day, too. I felt so close to you, Erica. The thought of losing you drove me into an abysmal spin. Thank God, you are alive and well."

Erica got up, hugged and kissed Jim.

"I am so sorry, I feel so bad. I know how much you would love to have a child."

"You are right. The inside of me is burning. Not only once, but twice I have been robbed of something so dear."

"Jim, there is nothing we can do now. At least, as the doctor told us, the miscarriage and the operation to clean my uterus won't interfere with my becoming pregnant in the future."

"Erica, we are so close. How come you never told me you were pregnant? You missed two periods."

"I wasn't sure. I didn't want to raise your hope. Besides, you heard what the doctor said at he hospital."

"What?" Jim asked.

"It's almost impossible to get pregnant if you are on birth control pills."

Jim was startled, got up, and hit his forehead with his right hand.

"Of course, I must be an idiot. I was so overwhelmed by the idea of having a baby, I lost it. After all, we had agreed to wait for two years before starting a family. How come you got lost? You made a left turn."

"I don't know Jim, maybe I was sleepy. It was dark. We've both had such a rough day, let's go to bed."

Jim went back to his office next day, and Erica two days later. Both hoped that the accident, after addressing certain legal issues, would be a brief and insignificant interruption in their unique lives.

Erica had to make up her mind pretty quickly, with her travelling and all, whether to settle out of court or go all the way for a jury trial, aware of the publicity could generate. She would discuss it with her attorney, but she knew the decision was ultimately hers. Jim had made it clear, he would go along with whatever she decided.

To begin with, there wasn't any question who was liable and the ability to come up with a big settlement. She and Jim were well off, and wouldn't be a matter of economics. Erica suffered no ill effects from the accident that would compromise her future as woman, wife or as a professional. What would be her motive for going to court? The thrill of victory. The ammunition and infrastructure were there. Why not use them? She lost the baby that would have made Jim so happy. Can his emotions be ignored? What she did for Jim before, why couldn't it be replicated again? One of the foundations of the legal system is the unwritten law of 'precedent.' Why not use it? What would be the downside of going to trial? Nothing, but losing a few days from work. And what would be the downside of settling? Everything; total surrender, and disavowal of a life-long commitment to always be in control. It was like a chess match where the offense was holding the same positions that had lead to victory before. Why not use them again? The same dynamics the same circumstances.

Are they? It all depends.

Mary Curtis, a highly successful attorney specializing in

family law, took the case and filed a lawsuit against the car dealership on behalf of the Woodmans.

Mary was a matronly woman, in her mid sixties, a widow and grandmother, about five feet six inches tall and on the plump side. Her hair was white and cut short. She wore either blue or gray suits with the skirt hemmed three inches below the knee. Her blouse was always white. She was known among court clerks as Miss. Drab. Her silver framed glasses, secured with a black cord, hung around her neck all the time.

She spoke slowly, quietly, with a disarming motherly inflexion in her voice. She was even tempered, but could be explosive at times.

Mary felt very strongly that Jim should be included as a plaintiff. The case was much stronger considering the fact that he had lost an unborn child before and the emotional impact it had. Mary and Erica, as experienced attorneys, understood the publicity and the media frenzy a trial of this nature would generate.

A pregnant, high class, beautiful, unusually intelligent, and successful corporate attorney - the wife of an executive and well known philanthropist - versus the wealthy owner of the largest car dealership in the city. The reckless driving of a sixteen-year old boy, the son of the owner of the car dealership, was responsible for Mrs. Woodman's miscarriage and the loss of the unborn child she and her husband had hoped for.

This was the dream case for any plaintiff's attorney, irrespective of legal expertise and temperament, that could bring the easiest pay off, ever!

Since the suit was filed four months ago, Mary Curtis and Daniel Peterson, the defense attorney for the company that insured the car dealership, had met only once. Liability was admitted and the insurance company was anxious to settle. The problem was that there was tremendous difference in settlement value between the two camps, based not only on economic factors, but on personal and philosophical considerations as well.

Daniel Peterson, five feet eight inches tall, lanky, in his late forties, was a man to reckon with. He always wore bow-ties, black, thick framed eyeglasses, and fine cowboy boots. He was known as the bow-tie cowboy, denoting his roots with a touch of elegance and formality. Out of the courtroom, he was polite, had good sense of humor, and was an excellent storyteller. His unruly golden hair covered part of his ears and upper neck. He had a tinge of a southern accent, and he could be tense, scrappy, crusty, annoying, and even sarcastic, but was always well-prepared and precise.

The trial was on the docket to start three months hence. Peterson was to meet with Curtis in her office this afternoon. He hoped it would be the last time, and that they would come to a sensible agreement. His appointment was for 3 o'clock.

He arrived three minutes early. The receptionist escorted him to the conference room.

"Mr. Peterson, Ms Curtis will be stepping in at any moment. Sir, would like a cup of tea or coffee?"

"No Madam, thank you, I'll just have ice water."

On the conference room table there was a pitcher filled with ice water and a stack of paper cups. Right in the middle of the table was a triangular teleconference telephone. High back chairs upholstered in burgundy leather surrounded the large rectangular oak table.

Peterson sat down, took out of his briefcase a thick folder and a yellow legal pad, and put them on the table right in front of him. He took a cup, poured ice water, and as he was taking the first sip, Curtis walked in. He got up, exchanged greetings with her, and they both sat down across from each other.

"Ms. Curtis, I hope today we can come to a sensible agreement and settle the case to the satisfaction of all parties involved."

"It's entirely up to you and your client, Mr. Peterson. The Woodmans, and especially Mr. Woodman, not only once, but twice was deprived of the opportunity to become a father, and the only thing you offer us is peanuts. Mr. Peterson, I don't think your client understands the gravity of the situation. You know very well how sensitive juries can be in cases like this. You cannot let a sixteen year boy loose to pick up any car he desires from his father's dealership, drive recklessly, and hit people."

"Ms. Curtis, every time we meet, you always talk about the jury. My gut feeling is that your mind is made up to go to trial, no matter what the offer is. I think you and your client want to repeat her last victory.

Ms. Curtis here is our last offer; two hundred thousand dollars, plus replacing her three year old car, with a brand new one of the same make and model. Your client has the option to take cash instead of the car, if she so desires."

"You must be joking, Mr. Peterson."

Peterson got up, angry but restrained, put his legal pad and folder back in his briefcase and started leaving.

"Mr. Peterson, where are going?" Curtis asked surprised.

"Ms. Curtis, I am extremely busy. I have a trial to prepare for. See you in court Madam, three months from today. Justice delayed is not justice denied. Have a nice afternoon, Madam," Peterson said and walked out.

There was no further communication between Curtis and Peterson. She was convinced that Erica's case was so strong that he would come back with a better offer, but nothing happened.

Ten days before the trial was to begin Curtis called Peterson directly.

"Mr. Peterson, this Mary Curtis calling, how are you?"

"Fine, Ms. Curtis, what can I do for you?"

"Mr. Peterson, our court date is ten days from today. Are you still interested in settling the case? Maybe we can compromise, up or down, and settle out of court."

"Do what? You must be kidding. Every offer made to settle out of court is off the table. You wanted a jury trial you've got it. Do you remember my last words when I left you office, after you tuned down my last offer?"

"No, I am afraid, I don't."

"I do, and I didn't even know how true they were then.

See you in court, Madam. Justice delayed is not justice denied. Goodbye now," Peterson said and hung up.

Curtis was totally bewildered with Peterson's behavior. She called Erica right away.

"Hi Erica, I just talked to Peterson and I am at a total loss. I thought, with the trial date approaching, we could sit down, negotiate, and meet somewhere in between his offer and our demands. He was so defiant I couldn't believe it. I know from your sworn deposition that he was obsessed with your left turn the day of the accident. Is there anything I should know or be worried about?"

"Nothing I can think of. As far as the left turn goes, I said it was dark, maybe I couldn't see. Even with all directions at hand and a map, we sometimes turn the wrong way and we don't know why. It just happens. I will see you in court. Goodbye, Mary."

The trial started as scheduled. The case of Erica and James Woodman-plaintiffs, versus Wheels Unlimited-defendant was assigned to district court # 2 with Judge Theodore Tolson presiding.

Tolson was strict, but a fair judge. He always expected attorneys to be on time and well prepared. His sentencing and judicial philosophy seemed to be idiomatic at times, but were well respected. He was a firm believer, that the punishment should not only fit the crime but the individual criminal as well, and that justice may be blind, but not inhuman.

Legal pundits were very critical of the defense for its lack of foresight in handling this case. They should have given in to the plaintiff's demands and never allowed the case to come to trial.

Some reluctantly questioned Peterson's participation and competence during the first three days of the trial. He allowed every prospective juror present to be seated with no objections.

He spent very little time or declined to question witnesses for the plaintiff.

Erica and especially Jim's testimony, on the third day, were devastating for the defense. When Jim testified expressing his feelings about the loss of his two unborn children, three women jurors cried.

After Curtis finished cross-examining Jim, the judge asked Peterson to proceed with his, but he declined, as he did with Erica. He gave the same response that surprised everyone attending the trial.

"The defense has no questions, your Honor."

The fourth day of the trial was the day everybody was waiting for.

Erica the Cool, the beautiful, the smart, the majestic, the super-lawyer, always in control, was to be cross-examined by the defense. This could be the courtroom scene of a lifetime.

The court session was to begin at 9 o'clock in the morning. By 7:30, every single seat was taken, packed with press and TV reporters. Judge Tolson wouldn't allow TV cameras in the courtroom, but they were outside. One TV station, Channel 7 Action News, would interrupt regular programs to broadcast, if any, breaking news from the trial.

Peterson arrived in the courtroom at 8:30. He went to the defense table and put his briefcase on top, and a three by six foot cardboard display with an enlarged photograph of a section of the city map. He took out of his briefcase an envelope with several photographs and a plastic bag with a pair of light brown color leather gloves inside and put them up in front.

Peterson took the enlarged city photograph and secured it on the tripod stand. The photograph, with a little adjustment of the tripod, could be seen from where the judge, jury, and the person on the witness stand sat.

On the enlarged photograph, there were six points marked with capital letters. Numeral A marked the garage exit from the Woodmans' apartment; B the 7th Avenue and Main Street intersection; C the Executive Athletic Club; D Erica's office; E the accident site; and F the Medical Arts Building.

Mary Curtis and the Woodmans arrived together at 8:55 and proceeded to sit at the plaintiff's table, which was to the right of the defense table. Both tables were across from the judge's bench, and separated by a corridor that led to the courtroom front exit, behind them. The jury booth was located to the right, and about twenty feet away from the plaintiff's table.

At exactly nine o'clock, the door behind the judge's bench opened, and as Judge Tolson was coming through, the court bailiff announced,

"All rise, the second district court is in session, the Honorable Judge Theodore Tolson presiding."

After the judge took his seat at the bench said, "Please be seated."

The court recorder who had set the equipment earlier close the witness stand, sat down and was ready.

The judge ordered Erica to take the witness stand, and the court clerk to administer the oath.

Erica got up, hugged Jim, walked to the witness stand with the utmost confidence, and as she put one hand on the Bible, and raised the other, the clerk asked her,

"Do you swear to tell the truth, the whole truth, and nothing but the truth, so help you God?"

"I do," Erica answered.

"Mrs. Woodman you may take your seat. Mr. Peterson, you may proceed with your cross-examination," the judge said.

Peterson got up and turned his head facing the judge.

"Thank you Your Honor."

Peterson took a few steps closer to the witness stand and asked Erica.

"For the record, would please state your full name?"

"My first name is Erica,(she spelled)E-r-i-c-a, and my last name is Woodman, (she spelled)W-o-o-d-m-a-n."

"Have you used any other names? And if you have, please state them."

"I have used Hofmeister, (she spelled) H-o-f-m-e-i-s-t-er, as my last name, which is my maiden name."

"Are you still using both names? And if you are, please explain."

"I do. Professionally, I use Hofmeister, my maiden last name. The reason is that my professional license was issued under this name."

"Please, state your profession, and your place of employment."

"I am an attorney, licensed in the State, and a member of the city, county, and state bar. I am employed by the legal firm of Moyar, Moyar, & Associates, P.A."

"Would you please, tell the court, what are your responsibilities with the firm, and if they have changed over time."

"I started in the trial division, and over three years ago I was transferred to the corporate division."

"Mrs. Woodman, would you say that your transfer was a big promotion?" Peterson asked.

Erica showed some discomfort, shrugged her shoulders, and lowered her head. Curtis got up protesting.

"I object Your Honor. The defense is patronizing the witness. My client's professional activities are irrelevant to this case."

"Objection sustained. Mrs. Woodman you don't have to answer."

Peterson smiled.

"Your Honor, I will come back to this later. Mrs. Woodman, as Erica Hofmeister, did you do any legal work for Mr. Woodman before you got married?"

"I object Your Honor. My client's legal work has no bearing on this case," Curtis argued.

"Your Honor, these two cases are identical. It's important for the court to hear Mrs. Woodman's personal beliefs as a plaintiff and compare them to her judicial philosophy as a plaintiff's attorney."

"Objection overruled. Mrs. Woodman, you may answer the question."

"My husband's first wife was killed in a car accident. She was hit by a city truck. At the time of the accident she was two months pregnant."

"Would you please explain exactly what kind of legal work you did for Mr. Woodman and how long ago it was."

"I filed a lawsuit on behalf of Mr. Woodman for the loss of his wife and unborn child. It was a little over four years ago."

"Was this case ever tried?" Peterson asked.

"It was not. It was settled out of court."

"Mrs. Woodman, settlement out of court, not once but twice, was offered for this case, but it was turned down. By coming to court and appealing to the jury's emotions, your hope is to make more money, isn't it?"

Curtis got up, and was furious.

"I object Your Honor, to this inflammatory questioning and remarks made by the defense, aimed to discredit my client, and her integrity in this court."

"Objection sustained. The question and remarks made by the defense are to be stricken from the court record, and the jury is instructed to disregard them. Mr. Peterson, I will not tolerate this kind of questioning in my court," the judge said.

Peterson picked up a document from the defense table, and raised his hand while holding it.

"I apologize Your Honor. Next time I will be more careful. Now for the court and the jury – and this is a public record Your Honor – I would like to read five lines from the petition Ms. Hofmeister filed on behalf of her client, Mr. Woodman, four years ago. Quote: 'Mr. James Woodman, as the result of this terrible accident that killed his wife and unborn child, sustained irreparable psychological trauma, pain, suffering, loss of consortium, and the prospect of becoming a father. The award for damages that were inflicted upon Mr. Woodman should be of value measurable to the loss of his wife and unborn child,' unquote.

Peterson walked to the witness stand, still holding the

document in his right hand, looked Erica directly in the eyes and asked.

"Mrs. Woodman, in this petition, not only once but twice you made reference to the 'unborn child.' At the time of the accident four years ago, Jennifer, the late Mrs. Woodman, was two months pregnant."

Peterson went to the defense table, left the document, picked up another one, and returned to the witness stand.

"Mrs. Woodman, four years ago, you believed that a two month pregnant woman carried an unborn child. Is your belief and conviction the same today as it was four years ago?"

"Yes, it is."

"Mrs. Woodman, you are consistent, and I respect you for that. Now I will go over parts of your deposition and the answers you gave under oath, when your attorney, Ms. Curtis, asked you:

Q: "Mrs. Woodman, please can you describe your feelings after your miscarriage?"

A: "I was devastated, as a mother to be, by the loss of my unborn child."

Q: "Mrs. Woodman, how far were you in your pregnancy at the time of the accident?"

A: "Two months."

Peterson pointed to the court recorder.

"Let the court record show the consistency of Mrs. Woodman's sworn testimony as a plaintiff, and her belief as a plaintiff's attorney that a two month pregnant woman carries an unborn child."

Peterson went back to the defense table, picked up Erica's hospital record, and returned to the witness stand.

"Mrs. Woodman, this is your hospital record. To make it easier for you, I underlined certain paragraphs. Please, for the indulgence of this court, tell us what the doctor asked you and what your answers were."

Erica, a little annoyed, glanced at the record, and handed back to Peterson.

"The doctor asked me if I was on any medication. I told him I was on birth control pills."

"You were on birth control pills. Is it fair to assume that your pregnancy was an accident and not planned?"

"But I'd love to have a baby. I was looking forward to being a mother."

Peterson, with a hint of sarcasm in his voice remarked.

"I don't doubt it, but you did not answer my question, Mrs. Woodman. I didn't ask you about baby love and motherhood. You evaded my question. You know better. You are an attorney, and a good one."

Curtis became furious, looked at the judge, and pointed to Peterson.

"I object Your Honor. The defense is attacking, harassing, and insulting my client."

"Objection sustained. Mr. Peterson rephrase your question, and keep personal commentary to yourself."

"Mrs. Woodman, the intent, the purpose, the pharmacological properties of the birth control pill is contraception. In other words to prevent pregnancy. Please answer yes or no."

"Yes."

"Is it right to assume, since you were on birth control pills, your intent was not to become pregnant at this time? Please answer yes or no."

"Yes."

"Isn't fair to say, since you admitted that your intent was not to become pregnant, your pregnancy was accidental and not planned? Please answer my question yes or no, and qualify your answer. You know what I mean."

"Yes, it was accidental," Erica answered.

Peterson took a deep breath in relief.

"Thank you, thank you indeed. The hospital record indicated that you didn't have a pregnancy test. Weren't you curious?"

"I was planning to. I had no symptoms except for two missing periods."

"Mrs. Woodman, had this accident not occurred, and your pregnancy had come to full term, how your professional life, considering your new responsibilities, would have been affected by having a child?"

"I object your Honor. The question is irrelevant and highly speculative," Curtis argued.

"Objection sustained."

Peterson with smirk in his smile and a sneer in face said,

"I was wondering, just wondering, Mrs. Woodman."

"Now, let's examine certain facts and circumstances surrounding the accident which occurred the 14th of April. The day before the accident, did you tell your secretary to cancel all your appointments between 9:00 a.m. and 11:30 a.m. for 4/14?"

"Yes, I did."

"Did you tell her why?"

"I wanted to go the club, and do my workout in the morning."

"What time did you arrive at your office the 13th , the day before the accident, and what time did you asked your secretary to cancel the appointments for the 14th the date of the accident?"

Curtis got up, and approached the bench.

"I object Your Honor. These questions are immaterial, irrelevant, and boring, to say the least."

"Your Honor, the defense intends to establish certain facts that may be boring to the plaintiff's attorney but very important to the defense."

"Objection overruled. The witness may answer the question."

"I arrived at my usual time, 8:30. I asked my secretary to cancel the appointments for the 14th at 10 o'clock."

"Mrs. Woodman, since you were in the office from 8:30 in the morning, was there any particular reason you waited until 10 o'clock, to cancel the appointments for the next day?"

"No, there was not."

"Mrs. Woodman, do you own a cellular phone and where do you keep it?"

"I do. I keep it in my briefcase. When I'm in the office it is connected to the charger."

"Do you use your cell phone to make outside calls while in the office, and if you do, how often; frequently, infrequently, never?" Peterson asked.

"Never."

"Neither do I. Now that we've established the chronology of certain events that occurred the 13th of April, let's concentrate on facts pertinent to the 14th of April, the date of the accident."

Peterson took a few steps away from the witness stand, stopped, made eye contact with the jury, then tuned around, and stared at Erica.

"Mrs. Woodman, how long have you been a member of the Executive Athletic Club?"

"About five years."

"Would you please tell the court the routine, and I repeat the routine of your workout schedule."

"Three evenings a week, after I leave the office. The club is on my way home."

"You stated you have been a member of the club for five years. How many times have you visited the club in the morning?"

"I don't remember."

"Mrs. Woodman, in order to enter the club you use an access computerized key card. Your entry, the time, date, and year, are recorded and stored. With a search warrant, we checked your records and found out that there have been no morning workouts, period. You are still under oath. I will ask you the same question you answered 'I don't remember.' Mrs. Woodman, how many times have you used the club in the morning?"

"Never."

"Thank you. Before we go any further, would you please tell the court if there was any particular reason the 14th of April, the date of the accident, you changed your routine for the first time in five years?"

"No, there wasn't."

Peterson approached the bench.

"Your Honor, I need more time. I would suggest the court entertain a recess, if Mrs. Woodman needs a break."

The judge asked Erica if she needed a break, but she declined. The judge ordered Peterson to continue with his cross-examination.

"Would you please tell the court, if you have a locker assigned to you at the club, when you use it, and what for?"

"I have one with my name on. Right before my workout, I change to my gym suit and shoes, remove my watch and my wedding ring, put them in my briefcase, and store my briefcase and my business clothes in the locker."

"Mrs. Woodman, on April the 14th, the date of the accident, you were already dressed for the gym, and your business clothes were found in the back seat of the car. Why?"

"I had planned to take a shower after my workout, and change to my business clothes before going to the office."

"That makes sense."

He walked to the defense table, picked up the pointer, and went and stood by the tripod where the city map was placed. He pointed the letter A first.

"Mrs. Woodman, this is where you exited your garage the 14th of April, the date of the accident."

Peterson continued moving his pointer, sequentially, from one letter to the next as he went along.

"You made a right turn, drove for about a mile and reached point B, the intersection of 7th Avenue and Main Street. Mrs. Woodman, if you turn right, in about three miles to your right, you reach point C, where your club is located. If you continue for another two miles to your right, you reach point D, the Trust and Commerce building where your office is located. From your apartment to go either to your club or office, you must turn right at the intersection of 7th Avenue and Main Street."

Erica for the first time appeared somewhat tense. She tried to conceal it with her usual aloofness and disassociation. Her eyes moved at random, and avoided making eye contact with either Jim or Curtis. It seemed as if opacity began to loom over her mind.

"Mrs. Woodman, I have a problem, a rather unsettling problem, that has been on my mind. I hope you can help me to see the light. To go to your club from your apartment, you must turn right at the intersection. This is the only choice; I repeat the only choice you had. Why in the world did you turn left?"

Peterson went back to the defense table and picked up Erica's pre-trial deposition. He carried it to the witness stand, put the thick file in front of her, pointed to it, and with a stern voice asked.

"Mrs. Woodman, when you were deposed under oath several months ago, you were repeatedly asked the very same question; why did you make a left turn. Why? Your answer was laced with vagueness, like 'I was lost,' or 'it was dark.' Since your deposition, have you thought of any rational reasons, other than vagary, that compelled you to make a left turn?"

"No, I have not," Erica answered with hastiness.

"Mrs. Woodman, you're a professional, intelligent, and well organized woman. For whatever reason you made a left turn, the wrong turn, that's fine. You went the wrong direction for about two miles, until you reached point E, where the accident occurred. Why didn't you turn around and go back before the accident?"

"I don't know."

Peterson, while moving the pointer away from E to F on the map asked Erica.

"From the site of the accident, and two hundred feet ahead, there is a four story medical office building, where the letter F is. Are you familiar with this building? Have ever been inside this building?"

"No, I have not."

"Is it possible, just a wild guess, maybe a crazy one, that something else was on your agenda the 14th of April, the date of the accident, that had nothing to do with visiting your club, but could explain and justify your left turn? Are you hiding something? Are you using your workout club as side alibi to cover up for an other location?"

Curtis became furious. She started walking between the bench and the jury booth screaming.

"I object Your Honor, I object. I object. This is an outrage. I move for mistrial."

The judge was mad. He looked at Peterson and in an angry voice said, "Sustained. Mr. Peterson, if you continue with this line of questioning, suppositions, and rhetoric, I will hold you in contempt of court. Stick to the record, and speak only from the record."

Peterson, with a sarcastic and indulging smile on his face remarked.

"Yes Your Honor, I will stick to the record, and speak from the record, but it won't get any better. It will get uglier."

Jim became upset and asked Curtis,

"Mary what's going on? What did he mean it will get uglier."

"I have no idea what Peterson is talking about. We have to wait and see. At least he made the judge mad. He will be more careful next time, I hope."

"Mrs. Woodman, your left turn is not the only problem I see in your testimony. There are other inconsistencies I hope you can help me understand and make some sense of.

You testified earlier that you take off your watch and wedding ring at the same time in the locker room at the club and put them in your briefcase, before you stored it in the locker. Inside your car, at the site of the accident and several miles away from the club, your briefcase was found open with your wedding ring on the floor, but not your watch, which you were wearing when you arrived at the hospital. What do you think happened?"

"I don't know. I cannot remember. It happened over a year ago. I guess I was planning to remove my watch later at the club and put it in my briefcase with my wedding ring."

"This is possible but highly hypothetical, and contrary to your routine. Since you gave a highly hypothetical answer, please allow me the same courtesy to raise a highly hypothetical question, too. Is it possible that removing your ring so far away from the club but not your watch, your intent was something else and not a workout, that you and only you know?"

Curtis got up, and in a very loud voice argued,

"I object Your Honor. This is a court of law. We deal with facts and not the 'Dialectics of Hypothesis.' The defense is trying to confuse the jury."

"Sustained. Mr. Peterson deal with the facts and get to the point."

"I will stick to the facts and get to the point your Honor, but the witness came with some preposterous answers, I was carried away, I guess."

"Mrs. Woodman, at the side of the accident, inside your car and by the open briefcase, in addition to your wedding ring, there were five $100 bills. Do you usually carry this large amount of cash with you?"

"No, I don't. Maybe it was left in my briefcase from my last overseas trip. I was in London over two years ago."

"You mean to tell me this money was forgotten in your briefcase all this time? It's possible, I guess anything is possible."

Peterson took Erica's deposition file from the witness stand back to the defense table. He picked up a plastic bag with a pair of light brown color leather gloves inside, went back to the witness stand, put it in front of Erica, and asked,

"Mrs. Woodman, can you tell us what is inside this plastic bag? Go ahead and open it."

"I object Your Honor. What tricks the defense is up to this time?"

"Please, approach the bench, both of you," the judge ordered.

Curtis and Peterson approached the bench. Peterson asked the judge to let him go the defense table to bring a document. Peterson came back with a copy of a search warrant and gave it to Curtis.

"Mr. Peterson, you may continue with your cross-examination," the judge ordered.

"Thank you, Your Honor."

"Mrs. Woodman, please remove the contents of the plastic bag and tell the court what is inside."

"It's a pair of light brown leather gloves."

"Can you tell, if it's man or a woman's?"

"Looks like a woman's."

"Do you own a pair of gloves like this? Could these gloves be yours? I want you to be absolutely sure."

"I may, but I am not sure."

Peterson went to the defense table, brought back a photograph, and showed it to Erica.

"Mrs. Woodman, this is a photograph of your car after the accident. Here is the right side, the side of impact. What do you see?"

"The right front pillar, with part of the fender and the door close to it are pushed in, and the right side of the dashboard is sort of buckled in."

"Oh my, you're a genius with laser eyes. You hit the nail right on the head. It took a few seconds for you, but it took several weeks for me, after I went over and over the same photograph. The police provided me with photographs of your car and a list of articles found in your car at the accident site, and the location where they were found. The list didn't include items retrieved from the glove compartment. Why? The dashboard was buckled in, and the door to the glove compartment was jammed! With all the commotion going on, and the effort to free the intersection to traffic, your car was towed to the impound lot without searching the glove compartment. With a search warrant, and two police officers present, we went to the lot, and using an ax, we opened the glove compartment door, and inside we found these gloves.

Mrs. Woodman, when I asked you before, while you were holding these gloves, if they could be yours, your answer was that you weren't sure.

I will ask you again the same same question. Could these gloves be yours?"

"Yes, there are mine," Erica answered.

"Thank you, Mrs. Woodman. I have no more questions."

Peterson approached the bench, and looked at the judge.

"Your Honor, the defense rests at this time. It is up to the indulgence of the court, Your Honor. We are ready to proceed with summation and closing statements."

"Mrs. Woodman, you may step down and return to your seat," the judge ordered.

As soon as Erica took her seat, the judge ended the morning session. The court was to reconvene for the afternoon session at 2 o'clock. The judge ordered all principals be on time.

The courtroom clock showed 2 o'clock.

The judge sat down and both plaintiff and defense camps were on a high alert mode.

Erica was quiet and pensive. Inside her mind, the chess paradigm had taken over. In a chess match with high stakes, utmost concentration and intensity go hand in hand.

The plaintiff's offensive strategy was to let the facts speak for themselves. It started with the premise that worked to perfection in the past; same dynamics, same circumstances, victory at hand.

The defense was aware of this and its inability to alter the dynamics. The only effective strategy would be to change the circumstances by redefining what the facts really spoke for. The defense needed only one unpredictable, unexpected, and out of nowhere move to win the match. Could this be possible?

"Mr. Peterson, you may proceed with your summation," the judge said.

"Thanks Your Honor."

Peterson got up, looked at the judge first, then at the jury.

"Your Honor, ladies and gentlemen of the jury, as I promised earlier, I will speak from the record, stick to the record, and stick to the facts. The defense never disputed the plaintiff's claim, that she was hit by an irresponsible driver and that her car was demolished.

The defense made every effort possible to address these claims generously and in a timely fashion. Why are we in this court today? Because the plaintiff elected to exercise her constitutional rights and have her claims heard and judged by a jury of her peers.

And what are the plaintiff's claims? Pain, suffering and loss of her unborn child. On April 14th the date of the accident, the plaintiff miscarried. She was two months pregnant. What are the facts, weighted not on the preponderance of evidence, but beyond reasonable doubt that occurred, the 14th of April or the day before?

Number one: On the 13th of April at 10 o'clock in the morning, Mrs. Woodman asked her secretary to cancel all her morning appointments for the following day, the 14th. Why? For the very first time in five years since Mrs. Woodman joined the Executive Athletic Club, decided to have her workout early in the morning and before going to her office.

Number two: At the site of the accident, the police searched Mrs. Woodman's car. By her open briefcase they found her wedding ring and $500 dollars in cash.

Number three: On April 14th, the date of the accident, Mrs. Woodman never completed her itinerary, never went to the club. Why? Because Mrs. Woodman made a left turn at the intersection of 7th Avenue and Main Street, instead of a right turn.

Mrs. Woodman never offered an adequate explanation, either today or the time she was deposed, as to why. The big question remains; was the left turn accidental or intended? And if it was intended, what was the intent?

Your Honor, ladies and gentlemen of the jury, we know exactly why Mrs. Woodman made a left turn, what the intent was, and we can prove it beyond reasonable doubt. The same Mrs. Woodman who came to this court to seek justice, deliberately made a left turn to keep her 7 o'clock appointment."

Erica started talking to herself.

There is no way. That's impossible. Nobody knew. How did he find out? This is unreal. Did Peterson find the unique defensive move on the chessboard that changes the circumstances to his advantage? If he did, the match is over. He won big.

Peterson continued;

"The same Mrs. Woodman, who came to this court to seek justice for the loss of her unborn child, at 7 o'clock on April the 14th, the date of the accident, she was scheduled to terminate her pregnancy by having an elective abortion!"

Pandemonium and commotion of cataclysmic proportions took over the courtroom, like an unexpected tornado that had fooled every knowledgeable and sophisticated weatherman in the entire country! It was like a volcano that erupted with vengeance after having been dormant for thousands of years.

Judge Tolson repeatedly pounded his gavel yelling,

"Order, order, order."

Curtis was screaming,

"Your Honor, this an outrage, unspeakable, dishonorable, despicable. I move for mistrial."

The judge called for one-hour recess, and asked security to vacate the courtroom. He allowed only the litigants to stay inside, and asked the attorneys for the plaintiff and defense to meet with him in his office immediately.

Outside the courtroom there was a media frenzy.

Everybody was on cell phones, screaming, yelling, and gesturing. A TV crew went to a live broadcast, and a reporter appeared on the monitor.

"We interrupt our regular program, to bring you breaking news from the Courthouse. Erica Hofmeister-Woodman, a well known, brilliant and beautiful corporate attorney- nicknamed the Queen of Torts from her old trial days – filed a lawsuit against the car dealership Wheels Unlimited for the loss of her unborn child. She was two months pregnant and miscarried after the owner's son, driving a company car, failed to stop for a red light and broadsided her vehicle. The defense attorney for the insurance company liable for Wheels Unlimited claimed he had evidence to prove that when the accident happened, Mrs.

Woodman was on her way to terminate her pregnancy. This is an unbelievable twist for a trial expected to end up with a high jury judgment. At the studio we have law professor and legal analyst for Channel 7 News, Ms. Liton."

"What are you making out of this, Professor Liton?"

"In any trial, late discovery is always a possibility. For any attorney to come up with such an accusation at the 11th hour, he must have credible evidence. The legal question remains though, how the evidence was obtained, and if it's admissible to this court. Several of my students who attended the trial were unimpressed with Peterson's performance during the first three days. He was just going through the motions, which is very unusual for him. He must have had something big up in his sleeve."

"Thank you Professor Liton. We will update you for any new developments from the Courthouse. Now back to our regular program. Jack Braden, reporting for Channel 7 News."

Jim and Erica stayed in the courtroom during the recess. They were visibly upset and kept silent. Curtis and Peterson went to the judge's chambers for a conference and stayed there for almost the entire recess. Curtis was the first one to come out the judge's office, walked to Erica and asked,

"Erica why didn't you tell me?"

"It was something so personal and agonizing. I was so sure. There was no way for anybody to find out. I was wrong. I am so sorry, Mary."

"So am I. We had it for sure, and we lost it. Isn't over until it is over. Too bad."

As Curtis was talking to Erica, the judge returned to the courtroom. The court reconvened and the judge addressed the jury.

"Ladies and gentlemen, both attorneys and I met in my chambers and reviewed the evidence the defense is about to present. The consensus was that the evidence was legally obtained and is admissible to this court. Mr. Peterson, you may proceed."

Peterson took from the defense table Erica's left glove, a folded piece of paper, and walked to the jury booth.

"Ladies and gentlemen of the jury, this is the left glove from the pair found in the glove compartment of Mrs. Woodman's car. Mrs. Woodman, under oath, admitted these gloves belonged to her. Inside this glove, the left glove, this folded piece of paper was found. When unfolded, what do you see? – Memo, from Ms. Hofmeister's desk – This piece of paper came from Mrs. Woodman's personal memo pad she keeps on her desk in her law office, and uses for inter-office communication. This memo has nothing written on, except what appears to be a telephone number, 562-7538.

A graphologist, a hand writing expert, analyzed and confirmed the phone number was written by Mrs. Woodman. The number was, and still is, listed to the Women's Health Clinic, located on the first floor of the Medical Arts Building, two hundred feet away from the accident site. Mrs. Woodman, under oath denied ever having been in this building. She lied.

On 4/12, Mrs. Woodman visited the clinic for the first time to be examined and have a pregnancy test done, which was positive. Mrs. Woodman, under oath, denied having a pregnancy test done. She lied. Mrs. Woodman paid cash for her visit, and was advised to call the following day to get the results of a more elaborate test to confirm she was pregnant.

On 4/13, the day before the accident, and at 9:30 a.m., Mrs. Woodman called the clinic to get the results of the second test. When she was told her pregnancy was confirmed, the procedure was scheduled for 7 o'clock the following morning, April 14th, the date of the accident. The clinic advised Mrs. Woodman to bring her health insurance card to check her benefits and coverage. She indicated she would pay cash and asked what the fee was. She was told $500 dollars.

Mrs. Woodman, testifying under oath, said she never uses her cell phone to make outside call from her office. She lied.

The cellular phone company records showed that the clinic's number was called on 4/13, at 9:30 in the morning, when Mrs. Woodman was in her office. Right after this call, Mrs.

Woodman asked her secretary to cancel all her appointments for the following morning, the date of the accident, and the date Mrs. Woodman had set aside to have her abortion.

The cash found in her car was not forgotten from traveling, as she claimed. She lied. The $500 cash found in car was the fee to pay for her abortion.

Mrs. Woodman, in her contacts with the clinic, used the alias Lola Brown. On the clinic's log of the 14th of April, the date of the accident, next to the name Lola Brown was written 'no show.'

Mrs. Woodman told the head nurse the first time she visited the clinic that she was single and out of town and gave as her temporary address Vista Hills Inn, 147 Cliff Road, a small country inn five miles out of the city limits. Mrs. Woodman reassured the head nurse that she would stay in the area overnight after the procedure, in case something happened.

Your Honor, ladies and gentlemen of jury, the evidence presented is overwhelming. A student of law might argue that the defense has failed to establish a link between Erica Woodman and Lola Brown. This was the easiest part of our investigation, considering we started with a phone number and nothing else.

The insurance investigator went to the inn and checked the guest registry book. Lola Brown was registered and supposed to stay, according to the book, on the 12th, 13th, and the 14th of April. In the space where vehicle registration and make were requested, it was filled in with 'Porsche' and Mrs. Woodman's license plates. This is the link.

The innkeeper told the investigator that in the twenty-five years he has owned the inn never experienced anything like this. It was like a fairy tale.

The most beautiful woman he ever saw in his entire life, with large piercing green eyes, walked in out of nowhere, paid cash for three nights in advance, and then vanished. Why? Mrs. Woodman had no intention to stay at the inn at all. She knew that in order to have the procedure done, she needed a phone number-she had her cellular, and an address-she didn't. To use her apartment address would have risked the anonymity and secrecy of her plan.

Your Honor, ladies and gentlemen of the jury, Mrs. Woodman lied, lied and committed perjury. All her talk and feelings for her unborn child was pure garbage."

Peterson moved closer to Erica and stared her in the face.

"Mrs. Woodman, if becoming pregnant at this stage of your career was inconvenient, it would have been within your legal rights to exercise your free choice option with the utmost secrecy and terminate your pregnancy. On the other hand, coming to this court as a grieving mother-to-be after your miscarriage while you were on your way to have an abortion, to say the least, you are intellectually dishonest, possessed by a devious, unconscious, senseless, and heartless mind.

Mrs. Woodman, I don't know you as person. You may be kind and caring. The insurance company offered you a reasonable settlement, but you turned it down.

You're wealthy and you don't need any more money, but when it comes to litigation, no matter where you stand, you become intoxicated with all the traits of a tigress, fox, and wolf combined. Victory means absolutely nothing to you. Only the size of the trophy counts.

Your Honor, ladies and gentlemen of the jury, the new discovery surfaced in the last three months after our final offer was turned down. The defense and the insurance investigators during this period of time tried very hard to find out why in the whole world Mrs. Woodman made a left turn. In the final analysis, our intellectual curiosity paid off.

Your honor, the defense moves that all claims for pain, suffering, and the loss of the unborn child be dismissed. The defense rests."

Erica on the outside looked emotionless, if not frozen. She felt the same inside for awhile. For the first time in her life she lost a chess match.

Checkmate, Checkmate resonated in her mind mixed with the

booming celebratory sounds of myriad of drums, coming from the camp of her victorious enemy.

After defeat, there are only two choices:

The first choice would be never to play the game again. If you don't, you are the living dead. Remember how Erica finished her valedictorian address in her high school? 'If you want to succeed in life, like in school, always do your home work, be prepared, *know your competitors*, have alternate plans, make no excuses, and *be ready to start over.*'

Erica either violated or forgot her own personal ethic and principles and that's why she lost. She underestimated her competition. If victory is always a given in one's mind, arrogance would take over that could impair sound judgment. Arrogance and its twin, Ego, have a subconscious communication line that constantly feed each other at the expense of virtue.

If the line between arrogance and ego is not controlled with relentless, unabated, and vigilant consciousness, it can become an abandoned high voltage electric line resting on wet soil – disastrous, incinerating, and even murderous.

The second choice would be to start over and go about your business the way you did before – taking chances and risking everything. Either you win big or you lose big. Erica tasted defeat for the first time in her life. She had a strong mind, and the mental power to survive. She knew her wings of gifts were clipped, but not cut off. She knew that she could fly again.

Could there be a third choice for her?

What about starting over with *rectitude*, the most powerful weapon, in controlling the self-serving feedback line between arrogance and ego?

Peterson, after his closing statement, sat quietly by the defense table. There was complete silence in the courtroom.

Judge Tolson removed his glasses, put them on the bench and addressed the court.

"The defense through intensive investigation cleverly conducted and properly and legally obtained, presented evidence to this court that changed the dynamics of this trial, and compels the court to consider alternate venues.

Mrs. Woodman, you came to this court as a victim and now you will leave as a villain. In the legal community, your are respected and admired for your intelligence, professional skills, and the uncanny gift not only to interpret the law, but dissect it down to its core. With all your assets you could become the standard and the poster child to be emulated by students of law for your jurisprudence and judicial temperament. You came to this court to seek justice by violating the most fundamental principle of justice; to tell the truth and not commit perjury. Mrs. Woodman, if you believed in the truth, we wouldn't be here today. You have to reassess your personal values and align them with the values of your profession and the oath you took to uphold them."

After the judge's comments, the court recessed for one hour. The judge, before leaving the bench, stated that when the court reconvened, he would pronounce his ruling.

As soon as the judge left the courtroom, the TV camera outside the courthouse went live; a reporter appeared on the on the TV monitor and announced.

"This is Channel 7 News. We interrupt our regular program to bring you breaking news from the courthouse. The defense presented evidence implicating that Mrs. Woodman was on her way to have an abortion, when the accident that caused her miscarriage happened. Our legal analyst, law professor Liton is on the phone. Professor, what are your comments?"

"Jack, this an unbelievable twist. You have to give credit to the defense and the insurance investigators for being obsessed with the plaintiff's left turn. The intent was to destroy the credibility of the plaintiff, and they succeeded."

"Professor, how do you think the judge is going to rule in this case, especially after the new evidence?"

"The expectation was, that the jury would have come up with a large judgment for the plaintiffs. Now they'll get nothing."

"What will happen to Erica Woodman now? Is she going to be indicted for perjury?" The reporter asked.

"She could, but not now, unless charges are filed. I know

Judge Tolson. He is innovative, intelligent, and very wise in his rulings. You never know."

"Now back to our regular program. This Jack Braden reporting for Channel 7 News."

The court reconvened on time. After the judge sat down spoke directly to Erica. "Mrs. Woodman, you came to this court as a plaintiff seeking justice and restitution for pain, suffering, and loss of your unborn child. Evidence presented to this court convinced me that these claims were fraudulent.

The lawsuit of Erica Woodman and James Woodman versus Wheels Unlimited is dismissed.

Peterson, with his thumbs up quietly said,

"Oh, yes."

The defense crew was elated. The courtroom became noisy as the media people started leaving in a hurry. The judge pounded his gavel on the bench several time and with an angry voice yelled,

"Order, order, be quiet. I am not finished yet. The court is still in session. Sit down, and be quiet."

Everyone sat down quietly, and silence prevailed in the courtroom.

Judge Tolson stared Erica in the face, and with a stern and resolute voice said,

"Mrs. Woodman, through calculated, convoluted, deceitful, and unethical schemes, and in violation of your oath before this court, you committed the despicable act of perjury. My language may be perceived as being invective, but I have no choice. Mrs. Woodman, when a lawyer of your caliber violates the law makes me angry. You lied under oath and you deserve to be punished. How? You are not a defendant in the court. What choices do I have? I could ask the prosecutor to arraign you for perjury and filing a false claim. If I do, you would plea bargain, your license could be suspended for a year or two, you could be asked to do some community work, and then you'd be back in business. I thought of something more sophisticated that would make you think and contemplate on what you've done every single day. Some will be critical of my decision and considered it invidious. This is my decision and I have to live with it.

Mrs. Woodman, taking into consideration that you are one of the most brilliant attorneys around, here is my ruling for you."

Curtis and Erica got out of their chairs and stood up side by side, as Judge Tolson started pronouncing his ruling.

"Mrs. Woodman, by the order of this court, and for the next two years, you shall be assigned to the public defender's office, and shall be responsible primarily for the defense of fraudulent and perjury cases, forging and passing bad checks, forfeiting loans and child support payments, attempted murder, etc.

Mrs. Woodman, by order of this court, your entire compensation as a public defender, shall be donated to the Women's Center, to be exclusively used for counseling and support of unwed young pregnant women, to help them make decisions and choices with which they can live the rest of their lives with neither pain, nor regret. Mrs. Woodman, do you have anything to say?"

"No, I don't Your Honor."

Then the judge asked Curtis and Erica to sit down and continued with his closing remarks.

"Mrs. Woodman, I think getting away from your high profile corporate practice will do you some good. By defending petty criminals, sometimes the scum of the earth, you will remember that once in your lifetime you were one of them.

Ladies and gentlemen of the jury, the court would like to thank you for your time and patience. Due to the new discovery, the law allows the court to rule alone without jury deliberation. Court is adjourned."

Erica, flanked by Jim and Curtis, tried to leave the courtroom as soon as possible.

Outside the courthouse, a large media crowd was waiting like starving vultures ready to eviscerate and devour the still warm corpse.

When they appeared, the attack began. Microphones

were pushed into their faces, like spears of Roman Gladiators, ready and willing to carry the defenseless, starving, emaciated, and infirm Christian prisoner to the Coliseum to feed the lions, and entertain the Emperor in Grand splendor.

A barrage of questions from the media crowd, in a rapid machine gun sequence, was heard.

"Mrs. Woodman, how do feel about the judge's decision?"

"Is your corporate practice over for good?"

"Mr. Woodman, how do feel about you wife's intention to have an abortion?"

"Can you trust your wife again?"

"Mrs. Woodman, do you want a child as much as your husband?"

"Can your marriage survive?"

"Some old buddies from your old court days said the "Queen of Torts" is back. Do you have any comments?"

Eventually they were able to pass through, and walked to the lot where Jim's car was parked. Erica hugged Curtis.

"Mary, I am so sorry, I didn't even think about the phone number on my memo paper until it was too late. Thanks for everything."

"You are welcome, goodbye and good luck to both of you."

Jim and Erica got in the car, and quickly left the courthouse parking lot. Jim drove for about six miles, and then turned right.

"Where are we going Jim?"

"I'd like to go to the park and get some fresh air. It's nice and quiet this time. It won't take more than fifteen minutes to get there. We don't have to get out of the car."

Jim parked as far away as he could and in a spot where there weren't any other cars.

"Erica do you mind if I open the window a little bit? It is not too cold."

"Go ahead."

Both were pensive and sat quiet for a while.

Jim kissed Erica on the left cheek once, then with both hands took Erica's left hand and kissed it several times. Erica was surprised, but no words were exchanged. Jim let her hand go, turned the ignition on, and drove home.

When they arrived at the apartment, both went to the bedroom. Erica took her clothes and her shoes off. She put a robe and a pair of slippers on, and went to the bathroom to wash her face. Jim took his jacket, tie and shoes off, and lay down on his back with both hands behind his head.

Erica returned the bedroom and asked,

"Jim, I am going to the kitchen. I am thirsty for grapefruit juice. Can I bring something for you?"

"No thanks."

Shortly, Erica returned to the bedroom, kicked her slippers off, went to the other side, lay down on her left side, and put her right arm across Jim's chest. Jim broke the silence.

"Erica, today must have been the worst day of your life and you are holding pretty good."

"Jim, it was, and it wasn't. Please hear me out. We haven't talked since we left the courthouse. I am sorry to disappoint you. I betrayed you and I lied to you. I was overwhelmed and overtaken by the responsibility of having a child at this time of my career. I wasn't ready. I love you and your love has changed me to a certain degree. Inside me the high gear is still fully engaged. Remember what Peterson said in his closing statement? Victory was not important to me; it was the size of the trophy that counted. He read me good. He was absolutely correct.

We had discussed it, how important the next two years would be for my career and you agreed to wait. On the other hand, I knew deep in my heart that if I became pregnant you would be delighted and excited. Jim, I never loved anyone before I met you. By being close to you, gradually parts of my female psyche have come into focus. That helped me to use my intuitive power as a woman to understand the man I am close to, the man I love. I sensed and knew that waiting was torturing you. You agreed only to please me. For you, it was a sacrifice. You were an expectant father four years ago, and the expectation has not left you. It has become stronger.

Despite my love for you, my impulse to be in control took over, letting nothing stand in my way that would interfere with my strategy and objectives. This has been my drive, my motto, and my ethic for as long as I can remember. Erica is always in control; why not? She is beautiful, smart, gifted, and fearless.

You asked me why I didn't tell you I was pregnant. We agreed to share everything. How could I share a decision with you that would have shattered the rebirth of your hope and joy? Was my decision to terminate my pregnancy, selfish, calculated, and cold? I don't know. How would I feel afterwards? Sad, guilty, neutral, happy? I don't know. Right now, I don't even want to think about it. Decisions of that nature are so complex, difficult and personal. Often, by being more critical and analytical, you reach a dead end, that freezes and scares you. My intent was there but somehow I feel different and maybe relieved, that it was done by somebody else, like the kid who hit me, and not me."

Jim turned on his left side, with his back facing Erica. He didn't mean to ignore or avoid her. His mind and heart were burning with the ferocity of an inferno. The closer Erica was to Jim the higher the intensity of the flames.

How could he? He was ready to explode emotionally. He gathered whatever power was left in him, and tried to maintain his composure.

"Erica, you said before that you betrayed me. You don't have the foggiest idea what betrayal is, and how visceral, tormenting, and poisonous can be. Betrayal comes from a sick mind and a dirty heart. You were an independent, successful, and intelligent woman, blessed with beauty and grace. You loved me and you became a given woman for the first time in your life to meet my emotional needs. I felt so guilty and so hurt to see you humiliated in court. I felt the lowest of the lowest on this earth."

Erica was surprised. She got up, put her pillow against the headboard, and sat on the bed.

"I brought the humiliation upon me, myself. I should have kept quiet and settle out of court. But no, this wouldn't be Erica's style. The opportunity is here, let's go for it. Let's go for another big trophy. Erica is always in control. This time didn't work. Erica was outsmarted. In court on the outside, I looked stony, unemotional, and lifeless. Later inside, I became intensely alert and sharply focused. My entire life was being played before me. Everything had come to me so easily all along. I was gifted. I saw parts of me I liked, parts of me I hated, and parts of me that scared me.

If life was a game, played on the chessboard, Erica never lost a match before. No checkmates for Erica, ever. Jim, in retrospect, I am glad I didn't settle. I would have never discovered frailty and vulnerability that are integral parts of every man's, or woman's life, no matter how intelligent, strong and beautiful they are. Jim, you didn't betray me. I betrayed you, myself, and my gifts."

Jim got up and sat at the edge of the bed, with his back still facing Erica and hardly able to control his tears.

"What you said doesn't make me feel any better. I am so sorry. I betrayed you much more than you could ever imagine. The immensity and enormity of my betrayal are of such colossal dimensions that even the deepest abyss cannot accommodate them. Erica, I cannot look you in the eyes anymore. My guilt suffocates me. There is no end to it, or relief on sight. My guilt suffocates me, and unabated agony has taken over. It feels like a monstrous and poisonous snake that immensely enjoys squeezing and biting you to death, never intends to kill you, but loves to perpetuate your torture with sadistic cruelty."

Erica moved and sat next to Jim, by his left side. She put her right arm around him and asked,

"Jim, what in whole world are you talking about?"

Jim got up, fell on his knees in front of Erica, put his head on her lap, and started crying and sobbing.

"Erica, I deceived you and I cheated you. I feel so small and worthless. I am so sorry. I don't deserve your forgiveness. I don't deserve to be with you. If you want to leave me, I wouldn't blame you. The judge, in passing, indirectly referred to you as scum. I am the scum for what I did to you. Oh God, forgive me, if this is possible. What I did to you was inhuman, conspiring, shameful, selfish, diabolic, venomous, pernicious, and intellectually dishonest."

Jim continued to sob. Erica was completely at a loss. She couldn't make any sense out of what Jim was talking about. She waited until Jim quieted down and asked,

"Jim, nobody is leaving anybody. Would you please tell me, in the name of the Lord, what is going on?"

Jim, still on his knees, took Erica's hands with his, and in a halting, quivering, and almost stuttering voice tried to answer.

"Erica, forgive me for what I did to you........I wanted...a... ...child so..... bad.....Oh my God......I.....I....cha......I.....cha.......I changed your birth control pills with placebo pills. That's why you got pregnant. Stanley and I are like brothers. I begged him. He didn't want to do it, but finally gave in and made pills to look like birth control pills. The last refill you asked me to pick up was a fake. Stanley felt so guilty. He called me back every day for three weeks and wanted me to go back and pick up your birth control pills. He finally threatened me; he told me he would call you the same evening if I didn't make the change. I did. Erica you were off the pill only for three weeks, but apparently long enough to become pregnant. Erica if you throw me out this very moment, I wouldn't blame you."

Erica asked Jim to get off his knees. He did, after kissing her hands again, and sat close to her.

"You know, on one hand we are so different, and on the other very much alike. At one point in our lives we became obsessed; you for a child and I for my career. For everything we do in life that ends up with victory or defeat, success or failure, there is always price to pay. It's up to us to discover the real value, and the redeeming power failure or success might have and their contribution to our growth as human beings."

Erica pointed to herself with her right index finger, and continued,

"Erica is still beautiful, smart, gifted, and will try to win, but not at all cost, and without compromising her intellectual honesty. Jim, for the first time in my life I discovered the redeeming power and value of failure; humility. Jim, your obsession liberated me. Otherwise, I would have continued to be the same old Erica always in control, looking for more trophies at any cost"

Jim and Erica were exhausted, mentally and physically. They laid down again holding each other, and shortly fell asleep.

CHAPTER FIVE

REDEMPTION

The trial was over Thursday.
Erica planned to go to her law firm office on Saturday morning to pick up her personal belongings.

She arrived at 7 o'clock, knowing that at least for the next two years, her high profile corporate practice was over. Was she upset? Not, really. Erica, a woman of resolve, had other things on her mind that she considered more important.

She sat down on her desk chair and tried to conceptualize the events surrounding the trial. She knew and accepted the fact that she had lost. Why? What went wrong? Her critical mind was consumed to find out the answer, but was blank. Erica's mind wasn't attuned to assess and analyze defeat, for victory was always a given.

She first took her diplomas off the wall and put them on top of the desk. Then, she opened the bottom drawer of her desk and took out a mahogany case that was part of her father's chess set, used for storing the pieces. She placed the case on top of the desk and opened it. She took, very carefully, one by one all the pieces from the chessboard and put them inside the case in order; on one side the black pieces and on the other the white pieces. She stared at the open case for a while, and started closing it, but suddenly stopped. Erica's face flashed, like a lightening rod and her green eyes sparkled.

She sat down, took the two queens out of the chess case, black and white, and put them in front of her. The queens, the most powerful and dynamic pieces of the chess game play against each other, and invariably determine the winner. In the process one will die, the other will live, or both will die or live, depending upon strategy.

It's a logical imperative that the strategy of each queen must be protected with the utmost secrecy. Erica's controlling mind did the unthinkable, the illogical, the unattainable, and the unnatural task; to command and control both queens and play the match from both sides of the chessboard. Erica went to court as plaintiff with the determination, aggressiveness, and the relentless mind of an attorney who always wins, and a woman who was always is in control.

Erica was happy, satisfied, and at peace with herself. She fully comprehended the logic and reasons why she lost the match. Two directives may determine the winner – choices of moves and timing of execution. Erica flunked them both in this match. She didn't even consider exercising the option to settle out of court earlier in the match that would have prevented the opening of Pandora's box, responsible for destroying her credibility and losing the match.

Erica left the office in an upbeat mood. Her precise, proactive, and quickly responsive mind made all necessary adjustments to ensure that her critical thinking and decision-making process would be always on a high alert mode from now on, never to be compromised again.

Human nature and vanity would never allow elimination of feedback lines of communication between arrogance and ego. One feeds the other. Nevertheless, alert and powerful minds are not only capable of disrupting the lines, but also of intercepting messages when necessary.

Erica knew when and where to start.

As soon as she got home went to her closet and found the box with her graduating class yearbook inside. She opened the box, took the yearbook out, and looked for her picture. After she found it, took a pen out of her purse and wrote two additions next to old ones written by one of her classmates.

Next to 'Ice Queen' Erica wrote 'has melted,' and next to 'Ms. Brain' wrote 'has a heart.'

❦

Later in the evening after supper, Jim and Erica went to the living room to listen to music, talk, and express their feelings. The CD they chose undoubtedly reflected the mood and inner thoughts of the moment: Verdi's Requiem Mass – a thunderous music of loss and entreaty, fear and faith, death and resurrection.

Jim felt completely responsible for reneging on his promise, and violating Erica's trust. He alone put her in the position she was now. Irrespective of what Erica said or believed, wouldn't lessen the intensity and the magnitude of the guilt he felt inside.

Erica was more philosophical. When something goes wrong, to assign a degree of guilt would be totally counterproductive. Her intentions went beyond Jim's violation of trust. She invented a plan of deception that compromised her integrity as an individual and as a trustee of the law. Erica never perceived herself as egotistical or arrogant. Maybe she was. Maybe arrogance and ego had become her second nature that could explain her modus operandi and controlling persona.

Erica knew that working at the public defender's office for the next two years wouldn't be that busy. It would give her more time to find out about her mind and her heart. She would try to capture important things that might have gone by unnoticed. Things, that went beyond beauty, intelligence, and wealth.

Jim and Erica were completely transposed while listening to the music. They sat on the sofa holding hands, like two lovebirds trying to support the other's broken wing. Alone, couldn't fly. Together could soar and conquer the skies as never before. It was up to them.

Adversity is like the high- intensity flame of an iron torch. It can cut through, melt and separate metal or it can glue it back together.

As soon as the music was over, Erica hugged and kissed Jim.

"You know and I know what happened over the past six days was a derailing event for both of us. What choices do we have now? We could be consumed by our lapse of judgment and mistakes, or learn from them and go on with our lives. If guilt prevails would become a destructive force that could impede personal growth and taking on new directions to avoid repeating mistakes of the past. Guilt's objective is to initiate constructive and positive changes. If guilt is allowed to persist beyond that point, it could become a paralyzing force and an excuse for failure. This is against our nature, and inconceivable for strong minds like ours. Jim, basically we are the same people, with the same heart and mind. As I said before, at this point, I cannot say whether my decision to terminate my pregnancy was right or wrong. Somehow, I feel relieved that the accident did it. My scheme though to benefit from it, was opportunistic, inexcusable, unethical, and immoral."

"What about me? I deceived you. It's all my fault."

"Jim, let's forget about what happened the last six days. What we had before is still in us. The uniqueness and depth our love and the promise to love with a sensitive heart and a powerful mind. Let's use them. From this moment on, let's promise to each other, that the last week's events, no matter how painful, will never be allowed to dictate and control our love, lives, hearts, or minds. This brief interval of darkness in our past should never be given the opportunity to cast even the faintest shadow on the brilliant horizon of our future."

"Erica, you are a great woman. I love you, I thank you, and I hope I deserve you."

Erica worked for the public defender's office for almost three months.

She tried to be as neutral and quiet as possible, playing the 'rookie' part very well. She toned down her fluent manner of speech and accepted whatever case was assigned to without asking questions. She came to realize that not only economics, but also intelligence and education grouped and stratified people in a society not by design, but by circumstances. The 'have' and 'have not' would be forever, irrespective of public policies, type of government, and political system.

Erica met and represented individuals, men and women, she didn't even know existed in real life, to be found only in dark fiction. She considered this part of her career as an internship in social studies.

Erica's first case was to defend a single mother of three for attempted murder.

The woman stabbed her ex-boyfriend in the stomach with a kitchen knife and almost killed him, after he hit her and demanded cash out of her welfare check she cashed earlier in the day.

The prosecutor, addressing the jury, lamented,

"An unarmed man was viciously attacked by this woman, with the intent to kill. His liver and intestines were cut. He underwent extensive surgery, almost died, and spent five weeks in the hospital."

Erica's plan was to make the jury understand that the woman acted in self-defense, not for herself, but for the safety and welfare of her children. In her rebuttal, addressing the jury she argued,

"Ladies and gentlemen of the jury, I don't know if you are bird watchers or devotees of wild life. Imagine a bird's nest with three chicks inside, shivering and hungry, anxiously waiting to be fed. The mother bird has just arrived at the nest carrying food for the little ones. Suddenly, a strange bird comes to the nest and tries to take the food away. The mother bird would do anything to protect her chicks, even killing the intruding bird. Some of you are mothers. You would never know what your reaction could be if your child was threatened. The mother's reaction, instinctively, in any society from the most civilized to the most primitive is to protect her child at any cost."

Erica's client was not only acquitted, but also she obtained a restraining order, barring the man from ever visiting the defendant's house again.

After the jury found the defendant not guilty, one attorney observing the trial mumbled,

"The Queen of Torts is back in full armor."

The surroundings of Erica's office were very humble, a far cry from her corporate legal practice office. She shared office space with three other attorneys, and all use the same secretarial pool. The pace was slow, and attorneys could leave early in the afternoon, unless they had a client coming in.

Erica left about 2 o'clock, went to the Mall to do some shopping and on her way home stopped at the florist to pick up the flowers she had ordered. Jim had a staff meeting and would come home for supper around 7 o'clock. That would give Erica plenty of time to prepare a nice supper.

She got home around 4 o'clock. She put the flowers, a centerpiece arrangement, on the dining room table, and carried a shopping bag to the bedroom.

Close to 7 o'clock, Erica went to the entrance hall and sat on the small loveseat, right across from the credenza. From where Erica sat could see the door. Her plan was to greet Jim as he came in, and before entering the apartment.

There was something different about Erica tonight. Her glowing face had an exclamatory quality that projected exhilaration and expansiveness.

As soon as the door opened, and before Jim had a chance to come in Erica ran to and kissed him.

"Welcome home, Jim. I love you. You are my life."

Jim put his briefcase on the loveseat surprised.

"Erica, I love you, too. What did I do to deserve this? You waiting for me by the door; it never happened before."

"It's not what you did, it's what we did."

"What do you mean we?"

"Be patient. You will see."

She took Jim by the hand and walked to the dining room.

"Erica, that's a beautiful centerpiece. It's the same one you had the first time I had dinner at your apartment. It was the day I came back from London, the day you picked up from the airport. I never forgot that day. It was the beginning of my new life. The birds of paradise look so fresh, but there are three not two like last time. You are such a good customer. Your florist wanted to be nice to you and gave you one more."

"Let's go to our bedroom. Give me your jacket, I will put it in your closet. You can change to something more comfortable for dinner."

Jim took his jacket off, handed it to Erica, and walked to the nightstand. He removed his pen from his shirt pocket, and on his way to put it on the nightstand, he suddenly stopped and pointed the pen to the headboard.

"What is going on Erica?"

Jim became somewhat confused, almost lost for words.

"Oh no, no, no!"

"Oh yes, yes, yes." Erica responded and started crying.

Jim reached and grabbed the Teddy Bear sitting on a baby blanket between the two pillows and resting against the headboard.

Erica kissed Jim several times, as tears started flowing out of her eyes.

"Yes, Jim. I am six weeks pregnant. I didn't do it for you, not for me, and not out of guilt. I did it for us. I don't know if you remember that the trial was over Thursday. Saturday, I went to the office to pick up my personal stuff, including my father's chess set. Once I put all the pieces in the case and closed it, it hit me like a bullet. A new match was to begin, and I was ready: Different dynamics, different circumstances.

As soon as I got home, I went to the medicine cabinet, and flushed my birth control pills down the toilet."

"Erica, I don't know what to say. Your are not only smart and beautiful, but you have a loving heart, too."

"Don't forget, the Ice Queen has melted and Ms. Brain has a heart. Right now my work is not demanding. By coincidence or by fate this is the best time for me to have a kid."

"To have a kid! Sounds so beautiful, so promising, and so loving. Who is going to be your obstetrician?" Jim asked.

"Jim, my gynecologist doesn't do obstetrics. Dr. Ferris, who took care of me after the accident, will be my doctor."

"When did you find out that you were pregnant?"

"I missed two periods. The second was due two weeks ago. I got a test kit from the drug store. It was positive. I saw Dr. Ferris this morning before I went to the office. He confirmed my pregnancy, and he wants to see me in six weeks. He said everything was okay so far."

"I would like to be with you when you go for your next appointment."

"Of course. I wanted to make sure I was pregnant before I got you all excited. That's why I went alone for my first visit. From now on we will do everything together."

"How strange life can be. Five years ago I was desperate, wounded, lost. Now I have everything I have ever hoped for, and even more."

"You said it, Jim. If life is strange for you, it's much more strange for me. Erica is married, and Erica is pregnant! Five years ago words like 'married' and 'pregnant' would sound cacophonous and dissonant to my ears, to say the least, and definitely not part of my conscious mind. We control our minds, and our minds respond to our will and logic, and the priorities we set forth. I think, at times, our minds are afraid of our hearts. I speak from my own experience. Jim in you, I found the love of my life. Our love will even mature and expand further with our baby. And you know what? My mind is not threatened, compromised, nor diminished. I think human nature would always like to find excuses for intellectual laziness, and for lazy minds blaming the heart is the easy way out."

"We are both so lucky," Jim said.

Jim was happy but subdued as Erica's pregnancy progressed.

He hoped and prayed that Erica would reach full term

without any complications. She was in her seventh month and everything looked good including her last sonogram. From the sonogram, Dr. Ferris could tell the sex of the fetus, but Jim and Erica didn't want to know. They wanted to be surprised. After supper, they went to the living room, sat on the sofa, and went about their usual routine; reading books about raising children, formulas, etc.

Jim all of a sudden put his book down, turned his head, and looked at Erica.

"This is crazy. In less than two months we are going to have our baby and we haven't talked or thought about names. How come?"

"I did, I did," Erica said laughing.

"You never mentioned anything about names, so I kept quiet."

"Tell me the names."

"I can't; that's my big secret."

"What about me? I don't I count?"

"Of course you do, as much as I do. I thought of the fairest plan to choose a name that would give each of us the same odds: fifty/fifty.

If it's a boy, you name him, Jim. If it's girl, I name her. If you agree, you better get started. I am all set. I have made my choice."

"That's fantastic. I am sure I know the girl's name and I love it. I hope I can find a boy's name that you would like, too."

"Are you sure, you guessed right?"

"Absolutely sure."

Jim picked up the book, thought for a while, and then went back to his reading. *Mary is a beautiful name, your aunt's name. She raised you. She deserves to be remembered. Coincidentally, Mary was my maternal grandmother's name. I love it.*

It's amazing, how certain events in the course of life, like expecting a child, change one's priorities and awareness.

Erica's mind with its segmented strategy put on hold all other activities and became focused on becoming a mother; not only physically through pregnancy and the anticipated birthing process, but intellectually by accepting the fact that having a baby would irrevocably change her life forever.

She knew that in a chess match, once you make a move you couldn't go back. Every move is final and may determine whether you win or lose. How did Erica feel? Did she make the right move? Would she win the match this time? When she saw first the beating heart in the sonogram and felt the first kick in her abdomen, she new her move was right and would be a winner, otherwise her mind wouldn't have committed with such will and enthusiasm.

Erica was happy but uncomfortable, as expected during the last month of pregnancy. She went on maternity leave from the public defender's office, and for the first time in her life felt the abandon of leisure.

The nursery was already furnished, with love, care and imagination, ready and anxiously waiting to provide warmth and comfort to a bundle of joy. Every day, Erica spent time in the nursery sitting on the rocking chair, contemplating not only the creation and development of physical life, but the creation and development of intellectual and spiritual life as well.

Parents from early on, anticipating the arrival of a child, go through all kinds of preparations to meet the physical needs. How do parents prepare themselves to feed the child's mind and help him or her develop their intellect and a loving heart? A child shouldn't be a live toy in the parents' playground, but a person with a mind to think and a heart to love. Erica believed that exclusive preoccupation and concerns with only physical needs, like feeding and clothing, etc., might starve and denude the mind and freeze the heart in the process. She and Jim were ready to provide the needed balance for an individual in the making. A child should be loved with depth, devotion, and the involvement of the minds and the hearts of the parents.

If love is guided only by sentiment alone could handicap

both. The parent and the child. The parent could become less effective and the child less responsive.

The last time Erica saw Dr. Ferris, asked him about the use of an anesthetic for the delivery. She wanted to be awake, but comfortable.

Dr. Ferris explained to her, that with either an epidural or spinal block she would be alert, witness everything and be free of pain. This type of anesthesia numbed the body below the waist, and was safe for both mother and child.

Erica and Jim attended Lamaze classes but Erica wasn't sold on natural childbirth. She never believed in fads, no matter how romanticized, but in scientific facts that had stood the test of time. She had heard many women started at natural, but some had to be put out completely. At least with the block she would see and hear everything, and with Jim next to her, pushing her stomach down, it would help the delivery.

Erica intended to breast feed the baby for at least six months. This was a fundamental first step that would provide tactile continuity of responsibility for the mother, and dependency for the child beyond the womb. She considered this very important for bonding, in addition to providing other physiological advantages, like passing certain antibodies that would help the baby's immunity against certain infections.

Erica, having been in control all her life and in command of her own destiny, was amazed how the mind gravitates to new axioms in assessing priorities and values to accommodate new entries and realities in one's life journey.

First, it was Jim. His entry into her life irrevocably disrupted, in the most positive way, her singular state of existence. Now it was the baby; another entry, another reality. Erica's mind, in an expansive and inclusive mode, accepted the new realities with joyous consent. Her mind felt neither threatened nor diminished. Why? Her heart and mind were in perfect harmony. Erica's intellect and drive to succeed were left intact, minus the subconscious dominance of her arrogance and ego to win at any cost, and the strategy to always control all the dynamics of all circumstances. Her public humiliation in court awoke part of her mind that she had suppressed for so long. It provided her with the redeeming power she needed to adjust and rearrange the balance of her values, in order to attain the present state of a tranquil, happy and consenting mind. Erica's serenity and inner-peace, designed by her own standards couldn't have been reached by sentiment and feelings of her heart alone, unless intertwined with the logic of her mind.

Jim was surprised with the objectivity, reality, and gallantry Erica, even in the last difficult month, had accepted her pregnancy. She maintained her independence, despite Jim's willingness to help. Jim believed that Erica was basically the same strong and independent person with enormous resources not only to adjust, but even thrive under the new order.

Her face still radiated beauty and her statuesque body balanced her pregnancy with pride, elegance, and style. Her maternity wardrobe was of impeccable taste, design, and fashion. Exhibitionistic vanity wasn't in Erica's armory, but if it were she could be a striking super model in any high fashion maternity magazine.

Jim's adoration and love, and Erica's reciprocal feelings made their love grow stronger and deeper. Both kept their promise never to externalized the deceptions of the past, the individual intent, weight, contribution, and guilt not withstanding, but to celebrate the present joy and look ahead to a higher level of integrated happiness that would go beyond and be devoid of personal flaws, shortcomings, and weaknesses.

Love without forgiveness, when betrayal is admitted and lamented for, is a shallow love. Shallow love is built on shaky foundation. Love built on a shaky foundation will fall. Fallen love taxes more than forgiveness unless was built on deception, selfishness, and lies. The power of love can reach its infinite state only if ego and pride do not impede the admission of wrong. Erica and Jim had the courage of admission. Forgiveness not only obliterated the wrong, but also liberated them from guilt to cherish love with new commitment and fortitude.

Jim's dream of happiness would hopefully become a reality soon. For the last nine months the void of so many years seemed to be filling in, despite the complexities of the past. The last time he experienced this kind happiness lasted only six hours, interrupted by cruel tragedy that killed his love. What he lost before became more and more distant everyday replaced by the touch and sound of what he felt and heard now. Jim's hands and the stethoscope on Erica's abdomen confirmed the gift of life; the vigor of a young body in waiting for them to hug, hold and kiss, and the hurried beating of a tender heart in waiting for them to love, cherish and adore.

Jim planned to take two weeks off once the baby was born. He wanted to experience and be an integral part of the entire process from the very beginning. He wanted to fill his mind with images, and saturate his heart with feelings that would last a lifetime.

It was 1:30 in the afternoon.

Jim had just returned from lunch, parked his car, and was on his way back to the office. While waiting for the elevator his cell phone rang - he answered.

"Jim speaking, Hi Baby. What is up?"

"Jim, I am in labor I called Dr. Ferris, and he told me to go to the hospital right away. I am ready to go. I will be waiting for you."

"Love, keep your cool and relax. I will be right over."

Jim returned to his car and drove home. Meanwhile, Erica sat on the loveseat in the hall, with a small suitcase next to her, waiting for Jim.

Within fifteen minutes Jim was home. He kissed Erica, picked up the suitcase, and both took the elevator to the main lobby. Jim's car was parked right outside the main entrance.

As soon as Jim started the car, Erica, although in pain, with a smile reminded Jim;

"Don't forget your promise. I hope you have picked a boy's name."

"I have, I have. I love your choice, if it's a girl. I hope you love mine, if it's a boy. Is the pain bad?"

"It's okay. I can take it. I am amazed with your confidence. We'll see."

Jim drove and pulled his car up to the admitting office entrance. A lady volunteer came out with a wheelchair, opened the car door and helped Erica, as the parking lot attendant handed Jim a claim ticket for his car.

After registration, Erica was wheeled to the elevator doors. The maternity ward was on the fifth floor. While waiting, Erica told Jim the pain was getting worse and suddenly her water broke.

After arriving at the maternity ward, Erica and Jim were taken to a maternity suite. A nurse helped Erica undress, put a patient gown on her and started an IV. She fastened wire leads on Erica's body and connected them to a TV screen to monitor Erica and the baby's heartbeat.

Shortly Dr. Ferris walked in, put a pair glove on, examined Erica as she lay in bed.

"Mrs. Woodman, everything looks great. You are progressing much faster for a first timer. Your water broke less than an hour ago and your cervix is dilated up to five centimeters. We are almost half way through."

"Ann, please keep checking Mrs. Woodman. When she is close to nine centimeters, move her to the delivery room and page me. Meanwhile, call the anesthesiologist to be available for the block, and give Mr. Woodman a scrub suit to change to."

Jim after changing to a scrub suit, pulled up a chair and sat to Erica's left. They looked at each other, holding hands, without saying a word. If their eyes could talk would speak volumes - Devotion, promise, happiness, a miracle in the making, and above all love. Tragic ending of one love was the beginning of another love.

Love never dies. Love is immortal. Love, in the infinite course of time, just moves from one frame to the next, to unleash its liberating power, unite, and heal wounded hearts and minds.

Unattended open wounds could kill. The healing power of love closes and mends wounds. With the passage of time love does not only make the scars smaller, but could even make them disappear all together.

It was 8 o'clock in the evening. The nurse, after checking Erica, called Dr. Ferris. The cervix had dilated to nine centimeters. Erica was moved to the delivery room, and after the anesthetic block was given and her legs were placed on stirrups, she was draped for the delivery.

Jim moved and stood next to Erica's left, facing her feet.

Shortly, Dr. Ferris came in after scrubbing his hands. He took a towel from a sterile tray to dry his hands, then picked up a gown, unfolded it and put it on. Ann, the circulating nurse, tied the gown in the back. Dr. Ferris put gloves on, and proceeded to sit down on a stool placed between Erica's elevated legs. To his right was the scrub nurse sitting behind the instrument tray.

"Mrs. Woodman, how are you feeling?" Dr. Ferris asked.

"I feel fine."

"Mrs. Woodman, the waiting is almost over. The head is fully engaged in the canal.

Mr. Woodman, please start pushing your wife's stomach down towards her legs. Use both hands. Imagine you are kicking a soccer ball and the net is stretched between your wife's legs. Aim right in the middle. Keep pushing.... keep pushing...I am rotating the head....keep pushing... keep pushing.... The head is out...Goal!" the doctor said laughing. Within seconds the baby came out, shivering and crying.

"It's girl, a beautiful healthy baby girl," Dr. Ferris said as he handed the baby to the nurse, after cutting the umbilical cord. The nurse placed a suction catheter in the baby's mouth and nostrils to aspirate secretions and mucus, cleaned and wiped off her face, and handed the baby to Erica.

"What a beautiful baby girl! Look at these deep blue eyes. Look at the brown hair. You don't see so much hair, very often, in newborn babies."

Erica kissed the baby girl and rested the baby's head on her neck and chest. Overflowing tears out of Erica's eyes reached and wetted the baby's hair like a sparkling crystal clear spring water feeding the sprouting bed of the rarest flower of all. The human flower. The only flower born with a mind to think, and a heart to love. How, when, and what the mind and the heart are fed with will determine how, when, and what the mind thinks and the heart loves.

Bearing and delivering a child is easy and physically predictable, with a predetermined life span like the sequence of a play: Scene 1, 2, Intermission, Scene 3, 4, then the end, with birth.

Feeding the mind and the heart of a child is difficult, unpredictable with a non- predetermined life span. Feeding has to be arduously customized to meet specific needs of each mind and heart in order to address individual and variable circumstances as they emerge, without variance or discord. If feeding the child's mind and heart were a play, there would be rapid scene changes, with no intermission nor ending. Physical growth is a given. Growth of a thinking mind and a loving heart are not.

Back to the maternity suite, Jim still standing was transposed to in an ecstatic state. Looking at Erica holding the baby close to her was an image that he wanted to keep vividly in his mind and heart forever. It was something emanating Divinity that inspired respect, admiration, and commitment.

Jim pulled the chair close to the bed, leaned over, put his face gently between Erica and the baby's, felt the warmth of both, kissed Erica and the baby, raised his head, and said;

"I thank you both. I love you both. Erica you gave me not only love, but something I had never experienced before; the sanctity of love. Kissing, feeling, and touching the warm and tender face of a newborn baby girl held by a loving mother is a spiritual event that supercedes all past accomplishments, successes, and individual happiness. This is the moment I have been waiting for and have dreamed of all my life. This is the moment that defines integrated and infinite love not as an abstract word but as an incarnated reality of divine origin."

A nurse, holding a clean blanket, came to the room.

"Mrs. Woodman, I will take the baby to the nursery now. We will bathe her, and put some clothes on. Later you can visit her in her bassinet. When it's time for feeding we will bring the baby back to you. By the way, the birth certificate is completed, but we don't have the first name yet. Have you decided?"

"Erica, it's your call sweetheart," Jim said hastily.

As Erica was giving the baby to the nurse said,

"Of course we have. It was so easy. There is one and only one name for a girl with deep blue eyes and brown hair: Jennifer. Don't you agree, Jim?"

"That's a beautiful name," the nurse said, and left the room with the baby.

Jim was totally surprised. He didn't say a word, and appeared completely dumbfounded.

"Jim, do you like it? Did you guess it right?"

"No, I didn't. Not even in my wildest imagination did I expect you to name our daughter Jennifer, after my first wife. Erica, you are a great woman, and so self-assured."

"Jim, if it wasn't for Jennifer we wouldn't be here today celebrating love and life. I never met Jennifer. She must have been a great woman. The way you loved her spoke volumes to me. I hope our daughter takes after Jennifer and us. Jennifer is going to be the Guardian Angel and the guiding light in our lives. The greatness of an individual like Jennifer endures and inspires love beyond previous personal relationships, place, and time. It's like a piece of exquisite art; it may change hands or residence, but it never loses its value."

"There never was or would be another woman that respects and admires her husband's first wife like you do. Why? Because you are a unique person yourself with your own qualities willing with an open mind and a loving heart to learn and appreciate newly found greatness without feeling insecure or threatened. Your capacity to change vision, and adjust your goals in life to accommodate new directions, necessitated by circumstances no matter how unpleasant and adverse might have been, denotes a person of steel will and sensitive character with depth, ready to recognize lapses in one's or another's judgment, and to forgive and forget. Erica, only people with powerful minds and sensitive hearts like you, can recognize and be inspired by greatness of others, without feeling diminished. In the final analysis the facts speak for themselves. Your intelligence and your decision making process are not devoid of principles and values. Rigid intelligence darkens one's vision. Flexible intelligence adds more lights in the search to discover hidden or ignored opportunities for happiness. The birth of our daughter today and the name you chose attest the capacity of your mind how to think and the capacity of your heart how to love. Erica, in the Universal court of Minds and Hearts today, and beyond reasonable doubt, you provided undisputed evidence that not only can you talk the talk, but also you can walk the walk, with your head up and full of pride.

Erica, my love, this speaks for both of us. To fall is human. To fall and get up is divine. In our life's journey, I hope and pray, that our love remains strong enough to keep us from falling, and if we do fall, strong enough to get us up fast. Our promise, on our wedding night, to love with a powerful mind and a sensitive heart should never be forsaken.

Let our minds and hearts remain on guard and stay united, virtuous and pure, becoming the clearing house for any intents or thoughts that would impede our finely tuned balance of communion within ourselves and with each other."

The day after Jennifer was born Jim went shopping. The neutral color in the nursery had to be changed to a little girl's room in a hurry. Erica and the baby were to come home tomorrow. For the first time the family would be together.

The word 'family' resonated a sweet melody in Jim's mind. Does sleeping under the same roof and eating together makes a family? It all depends on the hearts and minds. Physical signs of togetherness are irrelevant and may be discomforting and hypocritical at times, unless supported by hearts and minds committed to operate under a fully open communication mode guided by intellectual honesty and mutual respect.

Jim returned from shopping with a smile on his face and in an exuberant state of mind. He changed the white bedding in the crib to pink, and put a pink blanket in the small straw bassinet. He was happy that he was able to take two weeks off and planned to cherish every single moment. The waiting was so long, and the longing was so deep. He was glad they were over.

Erica and the baby were discharged from the hospital, late yesterday afternoon, and was their first night home.

It was 2 o'clock in the morning and feeding time for Jennifer. Erica had been awake for the last thirty minutes. She slowly got out of bed and tiptoed to the nursery. Within seconds Jim walked in behind her.

"Jim go back to sleep; there is nothing for you to do right now."

"It doesn't make any difference. There is nothing to do, but I can feel, and I can see. I can feel love, and I can see love. There is always plenty time to sleep, but never enough time to think and love. Sleep, no matter how physically necessary is, stops our minds from thinking, and our hearts from loving. If guilt or worries deprive us of sleep, why not let happiness keep us awake?"

Erica took Jennifer out of crib, kissed her tenderly, sat down on the rocking chair and started nursing her.

Jim pulled up a chair, sat next to Erica and started stroking her hair with his left hand and caressing the baby's feet with his right.

The light was very dim and the silence in the darkness was, on and off, rhythmically, hurriedly, and impatiently interrupted with fervor and determination by the fine suckling sound of the baby's lips attached to Erica's nipple.

Life gave life, and life will keep life going.

As Erica bent her head down to look at the baby, her shadow on the drapes moved, adding a mysterious and mystical presence in the nursery. A new life, irrespective of biological predictability, is still a mystery, for the heart and mind go beyond biological structure.

All healthy newborn babies have hearts and brains that physiologically and structurally are practically the same. Loving and thinking would not be.

What would make one heart to love and another to hate? What would make one mind great and beautiful and another dangerous and ugly? This shall remain a mystery until the end of time.

After she finished nursing, Erica changed Jennifer's diapers and put her back in the crib. Jim and Erica embraced, stared at the baby silently. Feelings of love, happiness, admiration, and wonder were mixed with feelings of responsibilities, sacrifices, and even fear.

Was it worth it? The question was more rhetorical and poetic than real.

Looking at Jennifer's rosy cherubic cheeks, her full of life body, and her beautiful blue eyes when open transcended the power of life bestowed upon mortals.

Jennifer, physically would be protected and had the potential, like her mother, to become a real beauty. What about the growth, and the beauty of the heart and mind? What about the ability to love and think?

Erica and Jim were tested, and their hearts and minds were committed to help Jennifer's heart and mind to become as sensitive and powerful as theirs. At least they would try. They were fully aware of the importance of making correct choices in life, driven by a sensitive and loving heart, and by a powerful and clean mind in full communion, which were necessary to protect the integrity and the purity of both and keep them unblemished and virtuous.

Erica, since started going to Jim's church, felt not only closer to him, but also became aware of other resources that would promote the balance and the dependability between mind and heart; spirituality. Spirituality does not only strengthen the minds and the hearts of individuals, bur also fortifies the links among the minds and the hearts of loved ones.

Minds and hearts, thinking and loving, must be bound together watching, supporting, complimenting, cherishing, and celebrating each other in a reciprocal state of uninterrupted communion.

If either the mind or the heart falters, gets sick, or seduced, and the other remains insensitive, neutral, busy, or indifferent both will suffer, if not perish.

If minds and hearts act separately, characters of values and principles couldn't be forged. If characters were forged without values and principles, would be defective and prone to self-destruction, directly or indirectly affecting others in the process.

EPILOGUE

In the course of life, despite sophistication, knowledge, preparedness, intelligence, and even brilliance two events would always remain elusive; time of death and the response of minds and hearts to various every day challenges, serious or not serious, for at any given moment the former maybe feeble and the latter capricious.

If there is a meaningful dialogue between the minds and the hearts would empower both with resolve, tenacity, and perseverance. Challenges, irrespective of magnitude, would be met and overcome easier with greater zeal, diligence and patience.

Certain parts of the story may have made you laugh, think, and even brought tears in your eyes. That's okay. You have a sensitive heart and your powerful mind didn't mind at all, for both work in concert.

Constantine-Dean A. Papas is a medical doctor, specializing in Vascular Surgery. He is certified by the American Board of Surgery and the Vascular Surgery Board, and practiced in Cleveland, Ohio for twenty-seven years.

After closing his office moved to El Paso, Texas where now lives with his wife Jeanne and daughter Leah, a college student.